# Clearwater's Redemption
## Tiffany Casper

**Wrath MC**

**Mountain of Clearwater**

**Book 7**

Copyright © Tiffany Casper 2021

All rights reserved. No part of this publication may be reproduced, distributed, or transmitted in any form or by any means, including photocopying, recording, or other electronic or mechanical methods, without the prior written permission of the publisher, except in the case of brief quotations embodied in critical reviews and certain other noncommercial uses permitted by copyright law.

# Acknowledgments

Cover Design: Tiffany Casper

Editor: Tammy Carney

My awesome team!!!

Chips Ahoy Chewy with Reese Cup Pieces – Thank you!

# Wrath MC

**Original**

**Clearwater Chapter**

Cotton – President

York – Vice President

Garret – Enforcer

Cooper – Sgt. At Arms

Xavier – Secretary

Dale – Treasurer

Walker – Road Captain

Knox – Icer

# Playlist

It Matters To Me – Faith Hill

Tennessee Whiskey – George Jones

Your Arms Feel Like Home – 3 Doors Down

I Don't Want To Miss A Thing – Aerosmith

Simple Man – Shinedown

Let Her Cry – Hootie And The Blowfish

Wrong Side of Heaven – Five Finger Death Punch

Come Join The Murder – The White Buffalo

I'll Follow You – Shinedown

# Table of Contents

Prequel

Prologue

Chapter 1

Chapter 2

Chapter 3

Chapter 4

Chapter 5

Chapter 6

Chapter 7

Chapter 8

Chapter 9

Chapter 10

Chapter 11

Chapter 12

Chapter 13

Chapter 14

Chapter 15

Chapter 16

Chapter 17

Chapter 18

Chapter 19

Chapter 20

Epilogue

A Note From The Author

Connect With Me

Other Works

# Prequel

## Wrath MC

The most notorious, dangerous, one-percenter motorcycle club isn't the one everyone knows about. It isn't the one everyone sees at rallies, charity events, or even at bars. Some say Wrath MC is just a myth. A club that was savage, a club that passed around women then sold them to the highest bidder. Others say the MC is full of nine to fivers and weekend warriors. They also say, no one wanted to cross them. Well, some of those myths just may be true. While there are rumors about the club and those are galore, the rumor of where the mother charter could possibly be located is the largest one of all.

The people in a little old county in North Carolina know better. The three hundred square miles in Clearwater held a secret. A very well-known secret or two. Little did they know, Wrath MC holds many more secrets, a lot of those are made of stories your momma warned you about.

Some people have even been rumored to have gone missing in the area, never to be heard from again.

While others have either passed through and are but a fading memory, some have come and gone and left their mark. While others have come and made their mark on not only the MC but on the community as well.

This story is about one of the members of Wrath MC—the Icer, to be exact.

Hold on for one wild alpha badass man and a romance that will last till the end of time.

"Expecting the world to treat you fairly because you are a good person is a little like expecting the bull not to attack you because you are a vegetarian." – Dennis Wholey

# Prologue

### Fiona Three Years Ago.

"Fried eggs two, bacon two, toast, and a side of house fries," I called out from the ticket I had just taken to Randy the cook.

"I swear," Novalie growled when she had to bring a plate back to the cook for the second time. "Customer says he doesn't like to have his food touching. We fixed that. Now his reason is his bacon is too crispy."

"It's customers like that one, that pisses me off," Randy said, I mentally agreed.

So while Randy was making the two orders, Novalie asked, "Hey, so what are your plans for Thanksgiving?"

Sighing I said, "Nothing really, my grandparents are going on a cruise."

"Well we are having a huge bash at the clubhouse; I would love it if you could make it?"

I've never been to a clubhouse; I thought about it over the next two weeks. Novalie was my friend, hell she was the only real friend that I actually had. So that morning when I had walked into the diner I had asked her if there was anything I needed to bring. Novalie had squealed with delight.

Since Novalie had been going through a lot of things, I hadn't mentioned that I had met someone and since I was just tired of being so alone, we had moved in together.

Sure things weren't great like any relationship, but what I didn't like was the fact that he rarely helped around the apartment cleaning wise and all of his income went to games and new gaming systems. Hello, we have bills to pay.

So here I was a week later, I walked out the door of our apartment while he had been playing video games. I had thought about asking Cole to come with me but something had kept me from doing it.

Especially due to what I had walked into last night after my double shift at the diner. I didn't even want to think about that.

The moment I had pulled up to the clubhouse, a man stepped from a shed that was at the front gate.

"Yeah?" I saw that his kutte had the word prospect on it. He had long blonde hair, a strong jaw, and a crooked nose. He wouldn't win any beauty contests but I could see the draw for some women.

"Hi, I'm Fiona, Novalie invited me for Thanksgiving," I said shyly.

"She said you were coming, drive on through. Have a good time." I gave him a small smile, then when the gate opened, I drove through, and spent the next five minutes trying to find a place to park.

It looked as if everyone and their mother had come here today.

Taking a deep breath, I hauled myself out of my car and tried not to be nervous. I looked down at what I had on, a tight long sleeve black shirt, a long suede skirt, and my light brown Minnetonka boots that came up to my knees.

Walking across the lot I looked at all of the bikes, but one, in particular, stood out to me, the paintwork on the gas tank, it took my breath away. It was a skull with a giant crow sitting on its head with its wings expanded. I freaking loved it.

I had done some research into my past, and I had found that a crow is the symbol of wisdom and divine spirituality with my people. Surprisingly, I wanted to meet the owner of this bike.

Walking to the big doors, I pulled one open. When I walked through there were masses of people in the huge wide-open space.

Looking around, I spotted Novalie as she had just set a dish atop a long bar that spanned the length of the right side in the room. I weaved in and through a throng of people, the moment she saw me she smiled and walked over to me as she threw her arms around me.

Returning her hug, I pulled back then smiled back at her. Standing there with Novalie I took everything in, in the clubhouse of Wrath MC. When you think about a motorcycle club, this right here, this is not what you imagine. Family gathered around heaping plates of food.

"So glad you came." I could hear the excitement in her tone.

"So am I. I needed this." I told her.

Cotton who had come into the diner to eat when she was on shift came up behind Novalie as he wrapped his arms around her, "Everything almost ready Kitten?"

I even swooned a little. He was handsome to the tenth degree.

"Yeah honey." She softly said, I had to look away, it felt as if I were ruining their little moment.

When she had told me that she was an ole' lady I had been shocked at first because I didn't know what that meant, until I had seen her man Cotton in his leather kutte. I had watched Sons of Anarchy; I know it wasn't really anything like the real world of a motorcycle club but still. Who didn't love Jax, Opie, and my squeeze, Happy?

"Yeah, just a few more things to take care of." With that, Cotton nodded and walked off.

It was nice to have someone to talk to and when Novalie turned her attention back to me, she gave me that look. She knew what that wrinkle in my brow meant, something had happened.

Without giving her the chance to ask, I told her, "So, you know how I told you about watching my pseudo grandparents and wanting to find that same kind of love?"

"Yes." She gave me a kind smile.

"Right, so I've been seeing someone. We even got a place together last month. Only I had been a fool. I walked in and he was sleeping with my sister." Novalie knew that Sorcha wasn't really my sister, just that we had grown up in the same orphanage when we were younger and we were both kind of taken in by two elderly people that we refer to as our pseudo grandparents.

Novalie scowled at me, "Now when you say sleeping do you mean…"

"Cole said they had only been sleeping when I left the next morning for work." I didn't try to hide the mocking tone. I had even crashed on the couch because I had been too tired to wake either one of them up.

"Girl, I've got some men at my back if you want us to mess him up," Novalie offered with a smile.

"Who are we going to mess up?" I heard Xavier ask, he had been on protection detail for Novalie quite a few times at the diner.

Novalie growled, "I'm going to mess you up, if you keep dropping into my conversations."

"Yeah, what are you going to do about it? You and your little self." He smirked at her.

I saw Novalie smile evilly as she called out, "Kane."

I knew who Kane was too, that was Cotton. I also knew that she was the only person on this planet that had the right to call him that.

"Yeah, Kitten," he answered her automatically, even though he was halfway across the room.

"I think Xavier here wants to go a round with you in the ring." The light in Novalie's eyes even caused me to chuckle.

"That right?" He asked as he turned fully to our little huddle.

"Fuck. Me and my damn mouth," Xavier muttered, I busted out laughing, the whole room erupted in laughter, all of them clapping his back as he walked away from us.

"No, it's okay," I murmured into my glass of sweet tea that the man behind the bar had just handed me.

However, just as I had taken a sip, I saw a dark shadow fall over us.

Turning my head it was to see a massive chest that was covered with a dark green t-shirt that sat underneath a kutte. I looked at his patch where his name was and saw that it read, Knox.

Looking up, and up which I had to crane my neck to do, since I was only five foot four, it was to find a man. A man that literally took my breath away, he was that gorgeous.

He had dark blue eyes, tanned skin, and full lips that I suddenly had to fight the urge to nibble on. He had a scar that ran along the right side of his jaw. Realizing I was staring, and realizing that he was staring right back, I dropped my head and took another sip of my sweet tea.

I looked at Novalie's wide eyes as she said in a timid voice, "Knox, this is Fiona. Fiona, this is Knox."

Turning my head to look back up at him, my eyes stilled on his arm.

Unknowingly I had flipped my wrist over, slid my shirt sleeve up and ran my finger along the Crow that I had tattooed on my inner wrist on my left arm.

I looked up into the eyes of the man that Novalie had introduced as Knox, I saw that his eyes had flared at the sight of my tattoo.

Without a word, he held his hand out for me. I heard an intake of breath that I ignored, almost as if there was some force driving me, I placed my hand in his, trusting this man.

Knox led us over to a table that was in the far corner of the room, he pulled out a chair for me, I was floored. No one had ever done that for me. I looked up at him in surprise.

Softly I muttered, "Thank you," as I sat my glass of sweet tea on the table.

I tensed under his stare with my hands between my legs. When I bit my bottom lip I heard him growl low in his throat.

"So.. um... what made you want to be in a motorcycle club?" I was getting nervous, and when I got this nervous I talked.

"Brotherhood." He whispered.

So I whispered back, "Just the brotherhood?"

"Men who think like me." He almost said it so quietly that I thought I hadn't heard him.

This man puzzled me. He didn't talk much, which I was observing when others walked by and tried to talk to him, but he never answered them, he just gave them a chin lift. But he was talking to me.

However, our conversation or whatever you want to call it was stopped when Cotton said, "Let's fucking eat."

Knox and I stood, then with him in front we made our way over to the bar, which he then, turned, held out his hand for me to step in front of him.

Suddenly I just couldn't help myself, nor stop myself from blurting out the words, "What do your crows mean?" I asked him as I looked up at him.

It was as if he could read my mind when he glanced down at me and muttered softly, "People."

His eyes never left mine, did he mean his family, or did he mean… that was when it hit me. People were moving out of our way not only because they respected him, they were afraid of him.

Just who was this man called Knox?

I filled my plate with Knox at my back and when I went to sit beside Novalie instead of heading back to the table we had occupied earlier, Knox had followed.

I chose to ignore the looks that Novalie, and Cotton had given him. He also paid them no mind as he sat his plate down, then walked over to our table, nabbed our drinks, then brought them back.

A few others sat down with us. I was introduced to York, Garret, and I already knew Xavier.

"Thanks again for inviting me Novalie, this food is great." I told her as I swallowed a piece of turkey.

"Girl hush. You would've done the same for me." She said as she dug her fork in her macaroni.

I felt a bump to my shoulder, I looked at Knox who had stopped eating as he looked at me with a raised brow. Why I found myself telling him, I didn't know. "My pseudo grandparents went on a cruise for Thanksgiving."

He simply nodded then waited. I sighed, "It's a long story. But I think this was the right decision."

When I said that I saw his hard eyes soften a degree then he continued to eat.

Conversation flowed around the table with Knox staying silent.

It wasn't until we had finished our plates, that I got ready to grab them to throw them away when I was stopped as Knox beat me to it.

He stood, grabbed them and our glasses.

I watched him with a curious frown as he tossed our plates, then he took his glass, and mine to the bar.

"Okay, this is fucking weird I've never seen Knox act like this." Novalie said with puzzlement written all over her features.

The others nodded as they too watched Knox.

But it was Cotton's reply that had me swallowing, "You hurt him, I'll kill you."

I froze, stared at him wide-eyed and almost walked out of the clubhouse to never look back, until a glass of sweet tea was placed in front of me, grabbing it I looked up at Knox.

He held his hand out to me, deciding I'd rather be with him then near Cotton, I stood.

When I placed my hand in his it was also to hear Novalie threatening Cotton. Smiling, I tossed her a grateful grin.

Then I froze yet again at the gravelly words that came from Knox's mouth, "You hurt her. I hurt you."

Knox then turned and led me out of the clubhouse and over to a swing that was nestled between two trees.

When he sat down, I followed him.

"Who's the asshole I need to handle?" I offered him a small smile.

"I walked in on my boyfriend sleeping with my sister, well she's not really my sister, we were brought up in the same orphanage until we were fostered together."

I heard the man growl.

"Cole, my boyfriend, he said they weren't doing anything, only sleeping. They had their clothes on, but still. It feels wrong." I ran my hand over my arm.

"It is. One woman. One man." Shockingly I knew what he meant.

"Yeah I know, I'd want my man to be pissed if I was merely sleeping in the same bed with another man."

He grunted in agreement with me.

"I haven't known him for long, only a couple of months." This made me sound like an idiot. Who moves into a place with someone else after only knowing them for a few months?

"Don't matter." No, I guess it didn't.

I looked up at the stars until I felt Knox's finger-tips tap on my wrist where my crow lay.

I figured he wanted to know why I had a tattoo put there. "When I was a baby, only two days old, I was dropped off at an orphanage with a blanket wrapped around me and a note that said, *'You are Apache. Forever embrace your warrior's heart'*. That was it. So when I got older and into a home, I had researched the Apache. I had read that a crow is the symbol of wisdom for my people, or wherever I come from. I don't know. I've always been fascinated by them, and I guess I just wanted to feel closer to my heritage if that's what it even is. I don't know why I just told you that." And I really didn't. I hadn't told anyone that. Not even Novalie, or Cole.

He simply nodded as he took a pull from his glass.

We just sat there underneath the stars after we had eaten, I talked about nothing important and he simply listened.

He had said a few words here and there, but to be honest it was how I felt in his presence.

It felt as if I mattered. As if someone cared about me.

And I knew that on some strange level he had. When he had told me to text him when I made it home okay, I had to tamp myself down so I wouldn't do a happy dance when he programmed his number in my phone.

I had been on cloud nine last night when I texted him that I had made it home.

And the one-word response I got was *Good*.

It felt as though I had cheated on Cole. Knox and I had only talked but there was just something about Knox that I couldn't get over. It felt as though I were tethered to him for life.

I never saw Sorcha again after that night that I had walked in on them in the bed sleeping. She had written me a letter that she was off finding herself, whatever the hell that meant.

Over the next few years I didn't text him often, mostly it was random at times. I texted him funny jokes I had heard, or when I'd had a really bad day at the diner.

I'd seen Knox in passing, and I saw him at Cotton and Novalie's wedding. Cole didn't want to come with me, but it was Knox that had stayed glued to my side, until he had gotten a text and left without a backward glance. He came to the diner for a meal three times a week. He was staying present in my life. He never spoke in the diner except to ask one question, "Okay?"

I hadn't been back to the clubhouse, no, Cole hadn't liked that I had gone in the first place without him. His words were, "I'm invested in this. No one is having you but me." Little did I know the extremes he was willing to go through to make that happen.

I still haven't slept with him, call me old-fashioned or call me a prude but I wasn't sure if Cole was the man that I was meant to be with.

All the times that Cole had tried to get me to make love to him, were about to reach their boiling point. Sure some of this was my fault. But then again, if a man didn't respect a woman's wishes, then he wasn't much of a man at all.

Cole hadn't really factored in someone else being in my life when I needed it the most.

"You have enemies? Good. That means you've stood up for something, sometime in your life." – Winston Churchill

# Chapter 1

### Knox Present Day

Walking into Dale's office on the top floor of the clubhouse, Dale hadn't said a word, just handed me a folder.

I tagged it, read over it, moved the sick fucks to the order I would end them all in. I saved the best for last.

Nodding to Dale, I left his office then walked down the stairs to the main floor.

Seeing Cotton, I held up the folder, and with a deep sadistic smile, he nodded.

Over the next four weeks, I hunted down the assholes that had wanted Maddox. Sick fucking human beings. The world was a better place without them.

I had places in certain states, where I handled business. Luckily for the others, I didn't have a place where they were located, but for this asshole, I did.

The sick fuck that was kneeling in front of me now though, I had waited for him. He was the bastard that had wanted Maddox.

I wanted him to be scared. The news of all of the others being taken out by my hand that had been involved in this, I wanted him to know that something was coming for him.

The others had died easily enough, but for this piece of wasted space, easy just wouldn't cut it.

Walking around my prey, smelling the acrid blood, I allowed it to fill up my senses. I thrived on that taste. The taste of revenge, fear, and of power. Here I had all the power.

And that all-encompassing power was something else, it caused everything else in the room to fade away.

I jerked the hood off of his head, as I said, "Shouldn't have tried to take the boy."

"I didn't take him." Funny that he knew which boy I was referring to.

"Shouldn't have thought about hurting that boy," I said in a deadpan tone.

The fucker didn't have anything to say to that.

"Shouldn't be doing anything to little boys or girls," I jerked at the chain that was attached to his wrists, pulling them up behind his back. I smirked when I heard both of his shoulders pop out of their sockets at the angle.

He howled in pain, "Fuck, man, whatever you want I'll give it to you, just fucking stop."

"Have the little boys you've hurt begged you to stop?" He didn't need to answer me, I knew they had. I knew they had cried through the pain. I knew how they felt.

My fury needed to be unleashed, but just a sliver of it, while he was still dangling I threw all of my weight into one solid punch to his temple.

His eyes rolled back in his head and he was out.

I moved the chain along the steel beam I had it attached to, when I had it above a steel slab, I lowered the chain.

I unhooked his wrists as I placed them in the cuffs that I had attached to the steel slab.

After I had his wrists cuffed, and then his ankles, I stepped back.

I walked to the one table in the room and grabbed a pair of pliers. Then I walked over to him.

With the pliers, I grabbed his flaccid cock with them through his jeans then I squeezed. His back bowed up off the table as he came too. Tears were leaking out of his eyes.

"Hope you like pain," I told him as I twisted the pliers.

Would you believe he fucking pissed himself? Shaking my head, this man was nothing but a little bitch.

It was time for me to have some fun. I pulled my knife out of its sheath at the small of my back, ran the blade over my fingertips, relished in the feel of the little bite that came along with it.

Snarling at him, I placed my gloved hand down on his forearm, then just like I was skinning a fish, I dipped the blade into his skin and slid it through his flesh.

His cries and howls of pain only made the monster that lived inside of me roar with happiness.

Sadly after that piece of skin came off, the fucker blacked out from the pain a-fucking-gain.

I walked out to the front porch and grabbed a bucket of rainwater, as I made it to him, I dumped it on his face.

He sputtered as he came to yet again.

"Fuck asshole. Fucking stop."

I said one word, "No."

After I had sliced off the skin on his other arm and his chest, I grabbed a screwdriver, put my gloved hand on his forehead to hold him in place, lowered to his ear, and whispered, "This is for Maddox." With a hard jab, I jammed that screwdriver into his eardrum.

I watched the life drain from his eyes.

After I stepped back I checked myself as I pulled the gloves from my hands then tossed them on the body, strangely I didn't have any of this vile piece of shits blood on me. Fucking A.

Being done with this piece of human filth, I poured gasoline on him, then on the entire floor of the wooden shack, grabbed my lighter, then lit the entire space on fire.

Taking another hit from my blunt, while I sat on my bike, I watched the orange flames as they engulfed the wooden shack I had found and bought under a dummy corporation.

I may be in an outlaw motorcycle club, but I hadn't gotten to where I was by being stupid.

Since I was done with these sick fucks, it was time.

In an hour I made it to Wrath Ink.

The moment Clutch saw me enter, he stood and nodded his head to his studio. He knew what I had done.

"How many?" he asked.

"Thirty-eight."

He didn't say anything as he got his shit ready, then he asked, "The bastards that kidnapped Maddox?"

All I did was nod.

"Fucking A brother." Clutch knew about Maddox because he was a member of our Dogwood chapter in Tennessee.

Clutch was also the only one I trusted to tattoo me. Even though I had to drive the five hours to have work done, it was fucking worth it.

On my right bicep, he tattooed thirty-eight more crows.

I've never told anyone the meaning behind the crows but my brothers only know what the crows on my right arm represent.

When I was a little boy, I had seen a crow fly down and attack its prey, mercilessly, I felt a kinship to them.

Hence why I now have around one hundred and fifty crows flying up my arm.

As I tried to pay Clutch he shook his head at me, "Nah brother, not for this." Nodding, I turned out of his studio and made it to the front door. All the while ignoring the women that had stopped what they were doing to watch me walk past.

Shit like this pissed me the fuck off. So fucking what if I was six foot seven and pushing close to three hundred pounds. So fucking what if I had ink all up and down my body, except for my neck, face, a portion of my chest, and my left arm.

However I noticed Shiloh at the end of the counter hadn't had eyes for me, but for Clutch, however, the man was ignorant of that fact as he walked to the women, ignoring Shiloh. Judging by her hurt expression, yeah she had it bad for him.

Since it wasn't my place and I needed to get back to Clearwater, Shiloh turned her gaze from Clutch to me, I nodded to her, then I watched a smile morph on her face as I walked out the front door to my bike.

I checked my phone before I got back on the road. I hadn't heard from her, which was unusual. She texted me randomly during the day.

To be honest, I didn't know how any of this shit worked. I was out of my element with this shit. In anger, I started up my bike and sped towards the clubhouse.

The moment I made it through the front doors, Cotton's gaze immediately went to the fresh ink that was wrapped on my arm, he looked me in the eyes and nodded.

Later on that night with my back to the rest of the club, I sipped on some Jack and debated on what the fuck to do.

I didn't mess with a woman that was taken. Hell, I didn't mess with any woman, at least not in the last five years. I hadn't seen not one woman that had turned my head.

Except for her.

"Knox, you need another drink?" I growled. Why the fuck couldn't Amberly take the fucking hint?

I held up my half-full glass of whiskey then brought it back down.

"Knox... I..." I knew what she was going to say, and I'd had enough.

Growling yet again I turned my head, "Done said it. Not repeating myself. Not changing either. Leave. Me. The. Fuck. Alone." I bit out at her.

It wasn't that Amberly wasn't beautiful, because she was, it wasn't that she had been with all of the brothers but me and Dale. It was simply that when I looked at her, all I saw was black and white. Not gray.

I wanted someone who was gray. Someone who didn't fit in either category. Someone that didn't give not one flying fuck what someone thought about her. Even though I was a big man, I didn't want a woman with a lot of curves, I wanted someone tiny. Someone that was also timid and shy, but yet that lit up with my touch, even though I'd never let her touch me.

And only one woman in all the years I've been alive has ever hit every single fucking one of those categories except the last one.

The club was alive at night like it always was. Lucy had the kids in the family room so everyone could kick back and chill.

"Hey girl, what's..." I didn't pay attention to her conversation, not until I heard her name.

"Fiona, honey, what is it?" At her name, I stood then walked over to where she sat on Cotton's lap, pulled out my phone to see if I had missed a text or a call, why hadn't she called me?

"Are you fucking kidding me?" Novalie asked in a growl, her eyes narrowing to slits as she listened to whatever Fiona was saying to her.

"I'm on my way. I'll fucking kill him." She growled just like a mamma cat.

"What?" I bit out in anger.

I ignored Cottons warning growl for speaking to his ole' lady like that. I cut my eyes to him, and at the look in them, I saw his eyes widen in surprise.

Novalie stopped her movements as she looked up at me with fire blazing in her eyes. "The bastard was in Fiona's bed with another woman, and when she went to leave, he fucking hit her…"

I didn't care what else she had to say. I threw my glass to the ground, hearing it shatter as I stormed out of the clubhouse, fury fueling me on.

That bastard had dared to put his hands on her. On mine?

Fucker was going to pay. Fucking hard.

"Don't try to be what you're not. If you're nervous, be nervous. If you're shy, be shy. It's cute." – Adriana Lima

## Chapter 2

### Fiona

Thanks to the double shift that I had worked for Virginia, my feet ached so bad that I wanted to lay down outside of the apartment building instead of walking all the way up four flights of stairs.

Did I care that god knows what is all along that sidewalk? Negative ghost rider. I didn't.

Inhaling a deep breath, I put one foot in front of the other and groaned at that first step.

The pain that had been in my feet had now radiated up to my thighs as I finally cleared that very last step.

Just the thought of taking my shoes off, taking a bubble bath, and drinking a little whiskey, made the pain in my feet and legs loosen just a molecule of the pain. I've never been a whiskey drinker, not since that thanksgiving day at the clubhouse. I had tried whiskey, none of it tasted right, not until I tried Jack Daniels Honey. Maybe it was that I really did like it, or it was simply something that made me feel closer to Knox.

Only, as I approached my front door, certain sounds were coming out of my apartment when there shouldn't be any.

What the fuck was that? Was my dog going ape shit again, I swear if he was, he was getting fixed immediately.

Ever since Cole had called and told me that the mess in my living room and the papers that had been on my island had been knocked off, I had wanted to beat Kida.

Kida was my fourteen-month-old, fifty-five-pound Lycan Shepherd. He had cost me a pretty penny, but ever since I had seen a picture of his breed, I had been hooked.

Kida loved me unconditionally, I had bonded with him when he was a puppy and the owner had told me that he was mine. Kida hated Cole though, we had been in too many arguments over that one. When I was working, Kida stayed in the spare bedroom.

Which was odd that Cole said the mess in the apartment was Kida's fault when Cole supposedly let him out during the day so he could use the bathroom.

I went to unlock the front door, which was odd, since it was unlocked already..

I walked in and that was when I saw a shoe. A red heel to be more accurate sitting on the floor beside my couch. Looking around I saw the other shoe, as well as Cole's shoes. A short red mini skirt soon followed, as well as a piece of black fabric.

That was when I heard the sounds. They were coming from the spare bedroom; no they were coming from my bedroom.

I dropped my bag on the end table nearest the front door, then not knowing what I was about to find, I went to the spare bedroom, opened the door and Kida came out, pushed himself against my legs, almost sending me to my ass, and then he started to push me, not in the direction of my bedroom but out to the front door.

I placed my hand on the side of his face and shook my head, my dog fucking huffed.

Walking to my bedroom, I pushed on the door since it was open a crack and what I saw had me wanting to puke.

There on my bed was a naked woman on her knees looking bored, but that wasn't what had my attention, no it was Cole who was behind her pounding into her, panting, and groaning.

I cleared my throat and Kida barked.

Cole's head snapped up and like a shot he pulled out of her, mind you, without a condom on.

I stared at my now ex-boyfriend as he scrambled off the bed, grabbing a sheet to wrap around himself while the woman grabbed the comforter.

I walked out of the bedroom, picked up the girl's things, and handed them to her. This wasn't on her. No this was on Cole.

"Not mad at you. Take your time." I told her. She looked at me with a confused expression until she saw the glare that I tossed Cole as I returned to lean against the entryway table with Kida at my legs while I waited for him to start his newest explanation.

Cole came out of the bedroom in a pair of pajama pants, and a wrinkled t-shirt.

However, I didn't really care about his explanation, not this time. "I want you gone, so I can pack up my stuff. Since your name is on the lease it's your place." I hadn't had good enough credit back then to put my name on the apartment but I had everything else in my name except the power bill which I paid anyway.

"You're not leaving this apartment. We are going to talk about this." Cole said angrily.

"Fine, I'll go, you let me know when I can come and pick up my stuff."

Kida was at my legs shoving me with his body away from Cole. Seeing that move Cole snarled menacingly at Kida. He better hope and pray that he never laid hands on my boy.

"Talk about what? The fact that you had someone in my bed not sleeping this time?" I shouted at him.

"Well had you given me that pussy, I wouldn't have had to." The smug arrogance in his tone and on his face, had me wanting to hit him.

I sneered at him, "That just proves that you're a piece of shit. Not every woman wants to have more than one man inside of her. I for one, only want one man and one man only."

"And you're a fool. You've got a good man standing right before you that does love you Fiona."

"You wouldn't know what love was if it slapped you in the face." I shouted at him.

I saw his face turn red. And then in the blink of an eye his hand shot out and he backhanded me across the face. Kida then stopped growling as he lunged at Cole.

Grabbing Kida's collar with seconds to spare I pulled him towards me, grabbed my bag and backed out of the apartment.

I didn't know if Cole would try to have Kida put down for protecting me had Kida gotten ahold of him, but it was something I wasn't chancing. Cole wasn't worth losing my baby.

I ignored the woman that was pulling her clothes on and making a beeline for the front door as well. "I didn't know. He told me he was single. I should have guessed that he wasn't because of all of the feminine things. And don't worry, you weren't missing anything, his dick is too small, I didn't even orgasm. Also from one woman to another, I admire the fact that you only want one man. If I could turn back time, I would do the same thing as you."

I nodded at her and as we all left the apartment as Cole started to shout yet again, but this time, Kida's hackles rose, and Cole wisely shut up.

As soon as I made it to my car, I dropped to my knees, placed my throbbing cheek in Kida's fur and sat there with my baby on the sidewalk.

There were only two people I would call but seeing as though Knox had barely spoken to me when I had texted him randomly, I called the other person, however, what I hadn't been expecting was that the person I had called had been in the same area with someone else.

That someone had come roaring into the parking lot on his Harley.

The moment the bike skidded to a stop, he tore his helmet off, and with an angry growl I saw fire in his eyes, he asked, "Where?"

I didn't want to answer him, but the fire in his eyes told me otherwise. "Apartment forty-four, top floor."

What shocked me was that before Knox walked up the stairs, he walked over to me and placed his finger-tips to my throbbing cheek. What shocked me even more was that Kida didn't growl at him, no before Knox pulled his fingers away, Kida licked them.

And then in a flash, Knox turned, then stormed to the entrance, threw open the door then disappeared from my sight.

I wanted to see what Knox would do, so Kida and I followed him up the stairs, only for us to never catch up to him.

When we made it to the fourth floor it was to hear things breaking and a man shouting and pleading.

"No. Look man… I.."

As soon as we made it to the door, it was in time to see Knox backhand Cole so hard his neck went sideways, with that momentum, he fell over the couch.

Not done with him, Knox bent, grabbed Cole's shirt as he hauled him with one arm over the edge of the couch. "Payback." Knox growled.

Cole wasn't a small man, he was six foot and around one hundred and ninety pounds, but he was no match for Knox.

And then he said in a low voice, "Respect a woman's choices."

That was all that was said as slammed Cole's face into his jean-covered thigh.

Just like that Cole fell to the ground in a motionless heap.

The entire time, Kida kept his body in front of me, making sure nothing could hurt me.

A few neighbors walked out of the doors, then peered inside my apartment and one woman said, "About time." Then she walked back to her apartment and closed the door.

"Grab your things honey. You're going with me." Knox said after he lifted his head, his nostrils flaring with anger.

"What about Kida?" I asked. I wasn't leaving him behind.

He looked at me, his jaw tightened as anger filled his eyes, "Your dog protected you. He comes."

Nodding, I grabbed my essentials with Kida's face low to the floor watching to make sure Cole didn't move.

Placing my three suitcases by the door, I grabbed Kida's things, and then like he was built of bricks, Knox grabbed everything except my bag, and a bag of Kida's things then he nodded for me and Kida to go first.

Once we made it to my car, opened my trunk for two suitcases, then my back door for the other, while Knox was putting them inside, I opened my driver's door for Kida to hop in.

As soon as I climbed in my car I looked at Knox. "I don't know how to thank you."

He looked down at me, his face softened as he said, "Give me you." touching my cheek yet again he growled, "Follow me."

I nodded as he closed my door.

His words ended up running through my head the entire drive. *Give me you.*

"Do not worry if others do not understand you. Instead, worry if you do not understand others." – Confucius

# Chapter 3

### Knox

The entire drive I kept glancing in my mirror ensuring that she remained behind me. I had a white-knuckled grip on my handlebars, fury still ran through my veins due to the mark the bastard had put on her face.

A few times I had seen her wiping away what I assumed to be tears. Bastard didn't deserve her tears. No one did.

After half an hour I pulled my bike up my drive. It was dark, so if someone didn't know where they were going, they wouldn't find it.

It had cost me a mint to pave the road on the mountain, but it had been worth it for my bike. And for my peace of mind.

Driving up the mile and a half incline the sight of my house standing strong and proud gave me a sense of satisfaction.

Most of my house I had built, except for the electrical work and the fireplace. I hadn't wanted to mess that shit up and end up paying more in a power bill.

I had built an A-frame-style house in the front, but the rest of the house was a three-bedroom three and a half bath. I had bay windows in the front that overlooked the front yard. I also had floor-to-ceiling doors that appeared as windows when the doors were closed.

Even though money wasn't an issue thanks to someone that I had met when I had been in juvie. There had been another boy there, one that had been in the wrong place at the wrong time. His Uncle had wanted his father's empire. His name was Jacob.

I had protected Jacob when others that were bigger than him tried to pick on him, I had been tall for my age and bigger.

Because of those actions when Jacob had been found innocent and had gotten out, he had taken over his father's empire. And a month later I had started to receive payments from him. Payments that I had tried to give back, only he wouldn't hear of it.

So I had used a small portion of it to build this house, and the other payments he sent through the years all went into an account that I haven't touched since then.

And every six months I get an interest payment of two hundred and fifty thousand dollars. And again every six months when that occurs I call him to tell him to take the shit back. Then I get hung up on.

When I pulled my bike to a stop in front of my garage, I hit the door for it to raise. Once I parked it I pointed beside my bike so she could pull in the garage.

"Leave them." I told her as she started to grab her things.

She looked at me as she nodded, then I walked around the garage that was attached to my house so we could enter the front door. Why I was excited to show her my house, I couldn't tell you. But her gasp when she saw the front porch was worth it.

"You have a front porch swing?"

The moment I turned on the lights, I heard Fiona gasp in surprise. I looked over at her to see her eyes wide as she stared up at the dark exposed beams.

"Knox, this… your house is amazing." I stood there leaning against a post as she took everything in. I watched her walk to the fireplace while Kida sniffed the area with her.

I felt my chest swell with pride as Fiona took in my home with Kida at her side.

"Your kitchen. Oh my god." She took in everything that there was to look at, and then I led her down the hall, where four doors were closed.

I wanted her to see my room, to see the room that if I had my way, she would be occupying. My bed was big enough so she wouldn't touch me when we slept.

Opening the door I said, "This is mine." I walked in front of her as she took in my room and then my bathroom.

Her eyes were wide. I had spared no expense with my bathroom, I had a walk-in shower that had ten nozzles, the tile floor was heated with a double vanity on the right side of the room. And against the wall below a tall window was a claw foot bath tub.

Just like I knew, she migrated over to that tub. "Use it." I muttered.

Her smile was blinding when she nodded.

I walked out of my bedroom across the hall to the only other room with a bed. "Yours." I said as I opened the door for her.

Turning on the light, Kida walked right in and jumped up on the bed. Guess he liked it.

"Bathroom." I nodded at her own.

"Get settled." With that I walked out of her room, went, and grabbed her luggage from her car and brought it all into her room.

"Knox, I don't know how to thank you."

Unsure how to accept the gratitude that she was giving me when I didn't deserve it I simply nodded.

An hour later I was sitting out in the backyard with the grill going. I had seasoned some steaks and had just put them on when I heard the sliding glass door open.

The first thing I saw was Kida as he ran for the backyard and took everything in. I saw him run the perimeter marking his new territory.

"Anything I can help with?"

I shook my head at her. I already had corn on the cob with the steaks on the grill.

"This is beautiful. How long have you lived up here?"

She walked past the grill as she too took in her surroundings. And what a picture it was. If I had it my way, this would be her and Kida's new home.

"Fifteen years."

"Who built the house?"

"Me." At my comment, her eyes widened as she looked at me.

"That really is amazing Knox, thank you for sharing this with me for however long." I wasn't going to tell her that it would be forever. No. Not until she got to know me.

I checked the food and seeing that it was done, I grabbed our plates that I had brought out here earlier that were on the outside patio, plated them, and then held up a steak for Kida as I looked at Fiona for permission.

"Absolutely. Thank you."

I held the steak out for him, ever so carefully he put his mouth on the steak as he pulled it from my fingers. Now that was a great dog.

He chewed once, twice then swallowed it.

As we sat down to eat after she grabbed two sodas from the kitchen I wanted to know about Kida.

"Kida?"

Her smile lit up the night sky, "I got him from a breeder in Virginia. When she had heard about my past, she invited me to come down and check them out. So I did. It was a blast. Kida had actually been slotted to go to someone else but it was fate. The moment I had walked into the area where she had all of the puppies, Kida made a beeline for me and refused to leave my side. Actually when I had thanked her and was about to put down a deposit for another puppy, Kida actually jumped the four-foot fence she had, just to get to me. Normally, they never let them go without neutering them to ensure the bloodline. But Kida actually snapped at her when she tried to remove him from my side. In my contract, I'm not to let him breed another female, and I am to bring him back in another year so he can breed with her females. I'll get one from that litter and then he will be neutered. If I fail that condition, she has the right to take him from me."

That would be over my dead body.

We finished eating in silence and I noticed that she didn't mind me being short with my answers. That was fucking refreshing.

While the crickets and the frogs serenaded the night sky I let the events from the day wash away. It was getting late, but she didn't seem to mind.

"Clubhouse tomorrow. Cassidee's birthday."

"I got her something. Normally Novalie brings her to the diner after so I can see her and Jasper."

Then she stood as she yawned and stretched out her back. Her ass was magnificent in the shorts she wore to work today.

Snapping me out of the vision that was in front of me she said, "Night Knox."

"Night." I told her as I sat there while she walked back inside to go to her room with Kida right at on her heels.

Unsure of however long I sat there, smoking a blunt I looked at the stars, going over everything I had to do for the next day.

Turning in I walked past her room and almost opened her door to see her. But knowing that it was too soon for her, I went to my own room and laid there for hours while she slept not even thirty feet from me. Finally.

"Suddenly this is all too hard. I am tired of putting up walls. I want someone with the strength - and the honesty - to break them down." – Jodi Picoult

# Chapter 4

## Fiona

After I climbed out of my car, Knox was standing there, I reached in and grabbed my bag.

Walking into the clubhouse felt so surreal, this time I was walking beside Knox. What I wished was that I had the right to claim him, to have my hands on him. To let everyone know that he was taken. What would it be like to have a man like him at your side?

And when other women stared at him as we walked through, it took everything in me to not growl at them.

"Hey girl." Novalie stepped up to me, I reached out and hugged her.

Through the years I had seen Novalie with her two children when they came into the diner to catch up.

"How are you?" she asked as she took in the bruise on my cheek.

"Taking it day at a time."

"Fiona, Fiona." I smiled down when I saw Jasper and Cassidee running towards me, grinning, I opened my arms and dropped to the floor for them as they ran at me.

Laughing I hugged them close, then when they pulled away, I grabbed something that I had found for Cassidee's birthday out of my bag.

"Happy birthday sweetie." I handed it to Cassidee.

"Thank you Fiona." She said in her little voice that was too cute for words.

"Your welcome sweetheart."

Once I stood back up, Jasper took Cassidee over to the gift table that was full.

"So let me introduce you to the ladies that have come to be a part of us that you haven't met before." I smiled at Novalie, and before I could follow her, Knox handed me a beer.

I grabbed it as I looked at him and offered him a smile.

There wasn't a person in the clubhouse that had missed that exchange.

The moment I sat down at a table that Novalie and a bunch of ladies were occupying, she started the introductions, "From right to left is Miriam, she belongs to Cooper. Phoebe is Xavier's. You know Lucy is Dale's, Valerie is Garret's. Marley is York's, and lastly is Sydney, she belongs to Walker."

The woman that Novalie told me was Valerie laughed as she said, "I think she means that they all belong to us."

I laughed as the other women chuckled right along.

"I need more candles. Creedence used my latest one last night when she took a bubble bath," Valerie shook her head.

Marley just grinned, "I'm putting new ones in the shop tomorrow, come by."

"I'll be there." Valerie said excitedly.

"Candles?" I asked Marley.

"Yeah, mom makes candles, she's been doing it for years." Caristiona grinned. She was a beautiful girl, I know that judging by appearances that Marley is too young to be her mom, it wasn't my place, but being that I wanted everything with Knox, I needed to get to know these ladies.

"Mind if I tag a long?" I asked Valerie.

"Absolutely want to meet me here in the morning and we can ride together?"

Nodding, Miriam even said she was coming with.

I had just taken a sip from my beer when Valerie asked the question I was sure was on a lot of their minds, "So what's going on with you and Knox?"

I looked over to where he was sitting at the bar. "I'm not sure." I told her honestly. "I should have left my ex a long time ago. Not because of Knox but because I had been a naïve fool."

"We've all been there sweetie." Lucy smiled, I adored her.

"Knox doesn't talk much, but the little things he does, it's like he lets his actions speak for themselves."

"Tell me about it. He never really spoke to me, but then he was buying our baby things and we had formed a bond. He even comes over to my parents' house for dinner once a week. Never says a word but he shows up if he isn't doing something for the club." Phoebe said.

"That's really nice of them to include him," I told her.

"I see him as my big brother and my parents see him as that as well."

Later on in the evening after the cake was devoured and presents were opened, the kids all gathered around for smores that Cassidee had wanted.

Standing outside with the women as they all told me how they came to be ole' ladies. And I knew right then and there that I wanted to be that for Knox. I had wasted too much time.

What I hadn't known was that Knox had kept an eye on me the entire time, he only moved when I moved.

After we had headed home, Knox had seemed distant and I wasn't sure what was going on. Not until I woke up the next morning and when I called his name, there had been no answer, only a note near the coffee pot. *Club thing. Be back tonight. – Knox.*

I dressed and met the women at the clubhouse. We all piled into Valerie's SUV as we headed to Marley's store.

The moment I walked in, I felt like I was in heaven. Marley had so many scents that instead of overwhelming the area, they all melted into one scent that was comforting.

"Love this." I said as I walked over to an elephant wax warmer. I knew that I would be leaving with one of them.

However, I bit my lip, wondering if Knox would be okay with me adding things to his house.

So I bypassed that elephant that would look killer in his kitchen and walked to the candles on the far wall. I smelled all of them as did the other ladies.

I had just taken a whiff of a hazelnut caramel candle when the roar of pipes filled the morning.

"Boys couldn't let us have a day." Miriam chuckled as the roar instantly cut off. I turned my head to the front door to see bikes that were backing up against the curb.

Wondering if Knox was with them, I shook my head, I wasn't his lady.

Turning my head back to the candle I saw that she had them in three different sizes, loving the smell so much, I added all three to the basket.

When the bell jingled above the door I looked as I watched Cotton, York, Garret, Cooper, Xavier, Walker, Dale, and Knox walk in.

All of the men went to their ladies, and I watched as Knox walked to me.

He looked in my basket, pulled the candle out, then he smelled it. He nodded, placed it back in my basket, then asked, "Only these?"

Deciding that I was going for this I walked over to the elephant warmer, grabbed it, then held it out to him, "Kitchen?"

Biting my lip in anticipation he looked down at me, grabbed it, checked it out, then he took my basket from me, placed the elephant in there and then he held his hand out for me to proceed.

I had to turn away from him so he wouldn't see the tears that were forming in my eyes.

Marley had the same scent of the candles in wax melts so I grabbed them too. Two packs to start out.

Picking up a roasted marshmallow candle I took a whiff, undecided on it, I held it out for Knox. The wrinkle in his nose had me laughing.

"Yeah, I created that when I was pregnant with Kiera. She laughed. "It's not everyone's cup of tea."

I was glad that she wasn't offended, she peeked in our basket, then she leaned around me and grabbed another one. After she handed it to me, I looked at the label, salted mocha. Smelling it I smiled then again held it out for Knox. He took one sniff, placed the lid back on then he proceeded to add it to the basket along with the other two sizes and two packs of melts.

Thinking that that was enough, I walked over to the counter so Caristiona could ring us up. I had just pulled out my cash when Knox handed her a fifty-dollar bill.

"Knox…"

"Our home." I stood there not seeing anything else. I didn't even notice the other ladies smiling and the men smiling. I didn't even notice that Knox had walked away from me until Novalie tapped my shoulder and pointed over to where he stood.

I felt my cheeks grow pink, "I've been there honey." She said with a kind smile.

Pulling a strand of my hair behind my ear I walked over to him.

With all of our bags in the SUV the men rode around us with three bikes in front and the other eight behind us, as we all headed to the clubhouse.

Turning my head it was to see Knox right behind where I sat.

Since Knox had to handle something at the clubhouse I headed home and started dinner.

Smiling when Kida met me at the front door. I let him out then I put the elephant wax warmer in the kitchen. I was right, it looked freaking awesome.

Hearing him pawing at the front door, I let him in, turned on some tunes, and started to make us some dinner.

Replaying today's events in my mind and smiling all the while.

"We must be willing to fail and to appreciate the truth that often "Life is not a problem to be solved, but a mystery to be lived." – M. Scott Peck

## Chapter 5

### Knox

Turning off the ignition, I walked my bike into the garage. Instantly, the smells coming from my home had my body being led by my nose all the way through the mud room and into the kitchen where I stopped dead.

Fiona was dancing to some music that was playing on her record player while she stirred something in a pot, then brought the spoon to her lips. When I had asked her why she didn't pull it up on her phone? I had received a glare, then she followed that up with, *nothing beats music on a record.*

I had to bend my head to calm my dick that was standing at full attention at the sight that beheld me.

"Hey, didn't know you were home." Her lyric voice sent shivers down my spine.

Lifting my head up, I nodded. What shocked me was that I had wanted to walk over there to her, wrap my arms around her and pull her into my body.

"Smells good." I told her as I tagged the beer that she had just pulled from the fridge for me.

The smile she gifted me; I would start a war for. "Dinners ready, hope you're hungry."

The moment the chicken hit my taste buds; I'd be willing to eat this every night of my life.

"Can I ask you something?" Looking up from my plate it was to see that she had pulled her bottom lip in between her teeth.

Wondering what was going to come out of her mouth, and what did, I hadn't expected that, "Can you take me for a ride on your motorcycle? I've never been on one."

I sat there as I contemplated what she was asking. How much she was asking for without her knowing it.

Coming to terms with something, I nodded, "Finish. Tomorrow" Before the ride I would run to town to grab her a helmet.

As she moved to grab the plates, I stopped her. "You cooked. I'll clean."

Her jaw-dropping to the floor had been a sight to behold. I allowed Kida to lick the plates clean before I put everything in the dishwasher.

The next afternoon, I took in a calming breath, I've never had anyone on the back of my bike. Just the thought of someone being that close to me again at my back caused me to freak out.

But she had asked this of me.

Taking in her smiling face was enough to get through this.

"Keep your hands on my hips. Don't move them." I warned her.

"Okay Knox." Nodding that she understood I walked the bike out of the garage, started her up and then shifted gears, tearing down the driveway with her squeal of laughter following, had a rare smile forming on my face.

Taking the back roads around Clearwater, I kept glancing in my rearview mirror and sure enough, she never lost her smile.

"Oh my goodness, can you pull over?" I heard her ask, slowing down, I saw that she was pointing to a field of dandelions, unsure of what she wanted but still wanting to see what it was, I pulled over.

She took off her helmet, handed it to me, then she ran into the field. Dancing to a rhythm that only she knew.

Pulling a blunt out that I rolled this morning, I grabbed my lighter, lit the end of it as I inhaled. Soon as I got a big enough hit, I quit with the lighter.

Sitting on the side of my bike with my arm resting on my handlebars I watched the woman that was slowly filling my cold dead heart.

How was she managing to do this you ask? While we were on a ride she asked me to pull over. To pull over next to a field of Dandelions.

Fiona was like nothing I have ever seen before. She embraced the little things. She embraced the simpler way of life. She didn't need much but what she gave, she gave a whole hell of a lot of.

I had been shocked all those years ago when she told me where she came from. Her hair was black but it wasn't box dyed black, no it was all-natural. When I met her in November her skin glowed. It wasn't from laying in a tanning bed or using tanning lotion to be something that you're not.

Plus her deep brown eyes that were set in a slanted frame. She had full lips that had a nude shade to them. I had only ever seen lips like that when I crossed into Indian reservations.

Fiona's heritage was Apache. That was all she knew. She had been dropped off at an orphanage when she was two days old with a note pinned to her baby blanket, a baby blanket she still has to this day. It had read simply, *'You are Apache. Forever embrace your warrior's heart'*. The note hadn't been signed. Nothing.

She had told me that she had researched her people. She even dressed in long floral skirts and she wore moccasins whenever she could. Today she had on a white skirt that was set just below her knees that was angled down. She knew we were going riding today so she had on a pair of moccasin boots that came up to just below her knees.

Her long black hair was braided so that her helmet would fit just right.

When she was finished, she had little white parachutes stuck to her, she exited the field with a giant smile on her face.

I was ready to have her on my bike. Not heading in one direction at all but just having her near me.

I had just felt rain drops hitting my cheek, glancing up I saw that the sky was about to open up, not that I minded riding in the rain, but I wouldn't be happy if Fiona got soaked.

However the moment we turned onto the driveway, the sky opened up, the trees helped block some of the rain but not all of it. I was just about to shift gears to get up the mountain as fast as possible, until I felt Fiona's hands leave my hips as she threw out her arms and started to laugh.

I couldn't help the small chuckle that revibrated in my chest.

After we parked the bike in the garage, I unlocked the door to the mud room, thinking she was right behind me but no, that silly woman was out in the rain, and I stared as Kida ran by my feet, out to her, as he too danced in the rain.

Had I known before the woman that she held closed off from the world, I would have stolen her from that asshole.

Once we were dried off and Kida had also been towel-dried I had just tossed our wet clothes in the washing machine and had just turned on the television after taking a sip of my Jack when I heard, "Knox?"

I turned my head to see what she wanted.

"Umm, well,….."

"What?"

I saw her biting her bottom lip as she seemed to be contemplating what she was going to say, normally, this shit really pissed me off. I was a straight shooter, but with her, I found myself patiently waiting.

"Can you umm… can you show me what I've been missing?" Her cheeks had turned pink.

At first I was unsure of what she was asking, until I looked in her eyes and saw that there was something in them. A fire. A passion. Something that she had held on to, wanting to let it out, but not for just anyone.

Without breaking eye contact I told her, "Be sure. Different. No touching."

I prepared myself for her to shake her head and say never mind. What I hadn't been prepared for was her to step away from the island and pull on the tie that held her day dress together.

Nor was I prepared for her to let the material fall away, only for it to reveal a body that I had dreamed of. Wondering what it looked like. Wondering what it would feel like beneath my hands.

Her breasts weren't big, no they looked small and perfect, just waiting to be treasured underneath that lacy black bra she wore. As my eyes traveled lower, devouring everything there was to see and searing it into my mind, I took in the matching black lace panties that she wore.

With emotion clogging my throat, I stood. "Bedroom. Now."

My dick was standing at full fucking attention. I had blue balls every single time I laid eyes on her.

"I'm dirty. Done a lot of things. Make fucking sure."

Instead of answering me, she stepped from her dress and turned her back on me as she walked out of the kitchen, disappearing down the hall.

I stood there for a few moments, gathering myself, the vision of her ass underneath those panties, I wanted to tear them off with my teeth.

Walking down the hall, I looked in her room, not seeing her there I headed to my room and sure enough, she was standing in front of the glass doors.

"Make very sure Fiona. You'll give me you. But you won't ever have me." I wanted her to know the score. I would take everything she had to give, but she wouldn't have that claim over me.

I saw hurt flash in her eyes before I saw it completely disappear. That single glimpse had me for the first time rethinking everything, but I would look at that another day.

"Do what I say." I warned her.

She simply nodded.

"Start by doing what's necessary; then do what's possible; and suddenly you are doing the impossible." – Francis of Assisi

## Chapter 6

### Fiona

Oh my god. Oh my god. Oh my god. I chanted again and again, had I really just done that?

Was I really standing in front of Knox in my underwear?

Would he really expect me to give him everything and expect me to not receive everything in return. But then I thought about all of the little things that he did. Maybe I could change that, not right now, not this day, but maybe another day, after all Rome wasn't built in a day.

He crooked a finger at me for me to come closer.

"Take off your bra." I hesitated for a split second before I complied. No one had seen me this naked except for at the orphanage when I had to be bathed until I was four.

Trembling as he advanced towards me I walked backward, trying to take cues from him, then when my back hit the wall Knox growled out, "Put your hands against the wall. Don't move them or I'll stop." Goosebumps raised all along my skin.

I felt his lips run over my collarbone, as he nibbled and sucked. I wanted his lips on mine but given that he didn't want me to touch him, I guessed that was out of the question.

But was I going to ask him to kiss me? No because, I never wanted him to stop, I never wanted to lose his touch, sure this was probably the only time I was allowed to have his skin on mine, call me stupid, but I would take whatever I could get from this man.

"Dreamt of these." I wondered what he was talking about until he pulled a nipple in his mouth, I almost dropped to my knees.

His hands never explored my body, but his mouth did. He let go of one nipple, then he attacked the other nipple. When my body was at a fevered pitch, he let go of my nipple.

I looked in his eyes, seeing something there that should have frightened me, but it excited me.

Suddenly, Knox dropped to his knees as I felt his mouth at my waist. He fucking growled as he grabbed my panties with his mouth and pulled them off with his teeth.

"Step." I stepped out of my panties.

And then before I could even think, Knox had his mouth between my legs.

It took everything in me to not react, to keep my hands on that wall. I wanted to run my hands through his hair, scrape his skin with my nails. I dug my fingers into his skin to feel his muscles as they pulsed and strained.

As his tongue moved from top to bottom of my pussy I felt my legs quivering. And then when he brought his tongue to my clit, I saw stars. My head lolled back as it smacked the wall but I didn't care.

The only thing that mattered was what Knox was doing to me.

And then I felt my climax as it rose and rose, higher and higher.

My body started to shake, and at his moan, I orgasmed, hard.

Knox didn't stop as he sucked my clit through my orgasm.

When the last of the shakes stopped, he stood, licked his lips, then unbuckled his belt, unsnapped his jeans, lowered his zipper, reached in his boxers, and pulled out his cock.

I looked down. The man was extremely well endowed.

I felt my eyes widen at the sight of him. He was gorgeous all over.

"Turn. Hands-on the wall. Bend forward until I tell you to stop."

I did as he said, hearing what I assumed was a condom wrapper.

"Stop." I stopped immediately.

Then I felt his fingers as he inserted one thick finger in my pussy, shoving it in, making me moan.

Then he inserted two fingers, I felt myself stretching around his digits. And then when his fingers left my pussy, I felt his cock head at my entrance. Ever so carefully he pushed forward an inch. "Stop?"

"No. Keep... going. God Knox. Please... don't ever stop."

Then I heard it, he had said it so quietly that I thought I had been imagining things, "Never."

Inch by inch he moved inside of me, moving in then backing out. He did this a few more times until I felt him stop. "Ready?"

I nodded my head, "Yes." I was panting.

Then and only then, did he push the rest of the way in. I felt a little pain as my hymen broke while I adjusted to the size of him in my pussy.

He stilled when he was buried full inside of me. Groaning, he started to move in and out of me. Hitting my g-spot with each shove. I was moaning and panting. The pain had ended, and now, I only experienced pleasure.

"Come." He demanded. It was as if my body was an instrument, being played by his hands alone, I came. My second orgasm ever given to me by Knox caused my back to bow as I moaned, my toes curled as feelings I have never experienced washed over me.

Then Knox moaned with me as I felt his entire body still. Looking up into his eyes, what I saw there, I wished I had a camera right then to capture that very moment.

"On the bed. Back." I walked over to the bed feeling the wetness as it ran down my thigh, climbed on, and laid on my back.

"Goddamn Fi."

I froze, "What did you just call me?"

"Fi."

I smiled, "Never had anyone call me that." I told him honestly.

As his eyes seared into mine he muttered, "Good." I watched as he took off the used condom, tied it, tossed it in a wastebasket beside his dresser, then grabbed another one, ripped into the condom with his teeth, I watched as he rolled it over his massive length so that I could have him inside of me again.

"Hands-on the headboard." I did as he said.

The moment he got on top of me, I moved my legs to accommodate him, with one brutal shove he pushed his way into me. I cried out as my pussy stretched yet again, but I was still so wet from what he had just done while he had me against the wall

With his fists planted in the mattress on either side of my head, he pounded into me. I lifted my hips meeting him stroke for stroke.

He pounded into me harder and harder, his eyes never left mine. With another thrust, my orgasm overtook any rational thinking. Within minutes, Knox came, groaning. "God fucking damn."

Smiling, I laid there underneath him, his skin still not touching mine. I would never regret Knox being my first.

I watched as he inhaled a few breaths then he slid out of me. I got up from the bed, headed to my own room and showered.

Just as I towel dried my hair, I walked out of my bathroom to see Knox in a pair of pajama bottoms standing in my open doorway leaning against the frame.

He nodded his head for me to follow him, curiously, I did. When I followed him into his bedroom it was to see that a line of pillows had been placed in the center of the bed.

"You sleep here. Move your things tomorrow."

Over the next few weeks every night Knox had me in some position or another, I still wasn't allowed to touch him. Even lying-in bed, he kept the pillow barrier up.

Sitting at the clubhouse one night I watched as Garret and Valerie had a little moment to themselves. The way he looked down at her, the way Valerie was allowed to touch him wherever she pleased, I wanted that. And when they kissed, I sighed. I've only ever kissed Cole. And even that didn't elicit the kind of passion that those too shared.

I knew I could have that with Knox, yes the sex with Knox was magical, but there was so much lacking that it wasn't even funny, and I wanted to experience it all.

But I also knew that Knox did things in his own time. I couldn't rush him. Even as badly as I wanted to.

I felt a shadow fall over me and looked to see that it was Phoebe.

"What are you thinking about?" She asked as she sat down.

I looked over at her. Then I looked around us to make sure what I was about to say couldn't be overheard.

Whispering, I asked, "How well do you know Knox?"

She chuckled softly, "I know as much as he will let me know."

Unsure if she was aware of this, "You know he doesn't allow anyone to touch him right?"

"Yes, but he only allows Bash and Pebbles to give him hugs." That was true, I had witnessed that on occasion.

"Well I mean, sex with him is all kinds of great don't get me wrong I'm so not complaining about any of that, he won't let me touch him but... well... he won't kiss me. It... I don't know..."

I expected Phoebe to show me pity and sadness but she just smiled, "Sweetie, the things I have seen that man do around you, are things I've never seen him do. That goes for everyone here. The fact that he even allows you to stand so close to him, that says a lot too."

"I know, he does a lot of little things that mean the world to me, but I just can't help but wonder why he won't kiss me."

"Ask him. You're the only one he really even talks to. Everyone else either gets verbal nods or one-word answers and even then that's a lot from him."

"I'm scared to push him."

"Why? Knox would never hurt you."

"Oh I know that. I'm just scared of pushing him too far and we lose the ground that we've made. Besides, there's so much more that I want to experience with him."

"I know what you mean. I gave birth to Maddox and I was still technically a virgin. My first time with Xavier I had been nervous, but I trusted him. He didn't break that trust. Trust in Knox. Maybe there's a reason why he won't kiss you, just keep giving him your trust and see where that leads you. Seems to me it's working okay so far."

However, when I had checked around us, I hadn't known that Knox was behind one of the wooden beams, listening to everything.

That night I sat on the porch swing with Kida lying beside me while I sipped on a Mike's Hard Lemonade, I rolled Phoebe's words in my head.

I had been watching the lightning bugs as they lit up the night sky when I heard the front door open.

Kida picked his head up and looked like Knox stepped out of the house and onto the front porch.

He took a sip of his whiskey as he walked over to me.

Kida immediately jumped down so he could sit and he went off to chase the lightning bugs.

The moment Knox sat down I took another sip of my drink. "Want to tell you something."

I looked over at him to see his eyes on me. "If you still want me, follow me after I'm through."

I nodded, "I'll always want you Knox. I doubt there's anything you could ever say to change that."

I heard him let out a deep sarcastic laugh. He tossed the glass of whiskey back and swallowed the rest of it. "Do you need more?"

He looked back at me, shook his head, and then when he spoke, he caused my heart to skip a beat.

"When I was four my mother let her pimp into my room, she locked the door. That was the first time I was raped. I had screamed, cried, and pleaded for him to stop, but he never did. Every other Wednesday I grew to hate.

That was the day that man would show up. I would bleed for hours afterward. Teachers never gave a damn, grew up on the wrong side of the tracks. And then when I was six, the man brought a friend. I ran away after that, however, that pimp had the cops in his pocket, every last one of them turned a blind eye. When I was seven I killed my first man. I wrapped a wire around his neck when he walked into my bedroom after my mother locked the door, she just wanted her next fix. The moment the last breath left his lungs, there was no other feeling quite like it. I went to my mother's room naked as the day I was born after that and smothered her in her sleep. Doctors ruled it an overdose."

Tears were running down my cheeks as I listened to him. I wanted to find those two, find a time machine, bring them both back and commit my own murder.

"Went to juvie for killing that man. Was there until I turned seventeen. Got out. Met Cotton. Told him the basics. He invited me to prospect. So here I am. The crows on my arm represent a life I have taken. When I had been sitting on the steps waiting for the cops to come I had seen a crow attack another animal. I felt a connection to them."

While he was telling me his story, Kida had sensed his duress, he had padded over to him, leaned his body into Knox's legs and gave him his support.

"Because of what that bastard did, I can't stand for anyone to touch me unless I touch them first. It makes my fucking skin crawl. But your touch. Your touch feels like a soothing balm. When your hand was in mine that first day, I had waited for the cringe, but it never happened. I've been with women, I ain't no saint, call it punishing myself, but I haven't been with anyone in seven years but you and I never allowed them to touch me, I never allowed them to go down on me, and I never went down on them. I always did them from behind. Never went back for seconds. I haven't kissed you because I don't know-how. Never done that." With that statement I knew that he had heard what I had told Phoebe.

I sat there as he stood, grabbed his glass, walked back into the house. I waited until I couldn't see Knox anymore, then I buried my face into Kida's fur and cried for him. What he had gone through. What he struggled with on a day-to-day basis?

If everything I gave him helped ease away his burden and sorrow, then he better be ready to take everything I have to give.

I grabbed my bottle, walked inside, locked the front door, on the way to the bedroom, I tossed my bottle into the trash can, then I walked to the bedroom.

Seeing him sitting on the edge of the bed, his knees bent, resting his elbows on his knees, his hands were on the back of his neck as he seemed to be lost in thought, it tore my heart to shreds. I also saw he hadn't put the barrier of pillows up yet, if that was what he needed then that's what he would get.

I walked over to him, dropped to my knees in front of him as I whispered, "I'll always want you Knox. Anyway I can get you. Your past doesn't define you."

After a beat he lifted his face to look into my eyes. I saw his eyes as they seemed to be searching for something, something that I wasn't sure of.

He nodded as he offered me his hand. I placed mine in his, he took a breath, then ever so carefully, he pulled my hand to the side of his face.

I watched his eyes close, felt his body tense underneath my palm, after a few seconds his body softened.

"I've only ever kissed Cole and I hated it. I know with you; it will be magical." Taking a deep breath I asked, "Do you trust me?"

He opened his eyes as he said, "Wouldn't have told you all that if I didn't."

Nodding I leaned in, made sure he saw what I was doing, I ran my hand over his cheek. "Do what feels natural Knox."

Without breaking eye contact until I was a mere breath away from his full lips, I closed my eyes as I kissed him softly. I felt his lips kiss me back, I couldn't help the smile. He pulled away, I saw his throat as he swallowed and the sight of my smile, had him bringing up his hand to run his palm over the side of my cheek, down to the side of my neck, and then he leaned back in.

He nibbled on my lips, exploring, I opened my mouth to give him better access and when I felt his tongue entire my mouth, I moaned. That was all Knox needed as he wrapped another arm around my waist, lifting me onto his lap.

I saw stars. My entire world felt like it had stopped spinning and it only consisted of him and me. Our make-out session didn't end until he pulled away.

"Sleep." I nodded as I climbed off his body, changed into my pajamas, and when I returned, the pillow barrier was no more.

Seeing him lay there with his arm out to his side, I looked at him, seeing what I was asking him, he nodded.

The moment I laid my head on his chest I sighed in contentment. "No one else but you Fiona."

Smiling, I nodded, "No one else but you Knox."

I didn't roam his body with my hands. Not yet.

"Too often we underestimate the power of a touch, a smile, a kind word, a listening ear, an honest compliment, or the smallest act of caring, all of which have the potential to turn a life around." ~ Leo Buscaglia

## Chapter 7

### Knox

When I awoke it was to find that I was wrapped around Fiona while we slept. Any other time, this would cause me to freak out, but with her, all I felt was being at peace.

This feeling, I hadn't had it since I was four years old.

Carefully, I untangled my body from hers, pulled the covers over her body, then I placed a kiss on her temple. It felt foreign to do that, but it felt so fucking right.

I dressed for the day, then headed into the kitchen to start a pot of coffee. I sat out some female chick shit I noticed she liked to use next to the coffee maker. Almond milk, and this hazelnut creamer shit.

As soon as the coffee was finished I poured a cup, black, then walked out to the backyard, while Kida's nails clicked on the hardwood floors behind me so he could do what he needed to do.

I still haven't told Fiona what takes me away from the house at different times. She didn't need to know about the number of deaths by my hands. Sure she could count the crows but still.

Since I had opened up to her, I didn't want to risk losing her. I hadn't gotten all of her yet.

Tomorrow night was the Bared Knuckle No Hold Barred fight night and I needed to get prepared.

After I finished with my coffee, left her a note, telling her I was headed to the gym.

Since Virginia had hired another waitress, Fiona's hours had been cut but she had to be at work in about two hours.

I didn't bother to wake her up, she was religious about getting up and getting to work on time.

Riding into the clubhouse I pulled my bike around to the side of the garage. Behind it sat the old garage that Cotton transformed into a gym for everyone to use. We had all pitched in to buy the equipment.

I had just laid down on the bench to start on my reps and started to bench press four fifty when Garret walked in.

He saw me, checked my weights, and smirked, shaking his head he muttered, "Valerie's going to be pissed I get my face bashed in."

"Then don't." I shrugged.

He laughed, "Brother you hit fucking hard."

And Garret wasn't a slouch either, he hit just as hard with certain punches.

As the other men filed in I started with my weights.

"Brother, got a Dove, need you to go get her, take her to a secure location."

Sighing I nodded, finished with my weights and then I stood. Went to my room in the clubhouse, showered, and changed.

When I made it to Dale, I grabbed the file, then I headed to the diner to let Fiona know what was going on.

The moment I parked the SUV that we used for this job it was to see that everyone and their mother had come to the diner this morning.

Opening the door, I walked in, she was walking around filling cups of coffee.

When she looked up, I saw her eyes widen. Then that killer smile broke out on her face.

The moment she made it over to me I leaned in, "Got business with the club. Won't be home tonight."

"Okay. Girls and I have a girl day before the fights."

Nodding, "Alarm system. Keep Kida near you."

She smiled, leaned in, and kissed my cheek. "Be careful."

Six hours later when I made it to the location on the file, there was a woman holding a baby sitting outside of a restaurant.

"Colette?" I asked her.

She saw the kutte I had on when I had stepped from the SUV. She nodded then stood as she walked over

I watched as her eyes ate me up which caused my skin to crawl. "Yes, thank god. I've been so scared."

After she loaded the baby up in the car seat that we had in the back, she moved to hug me, "No touching."

I climbed in the SUV and saw that she had a dark scowl on her face. What the fuck?

My phone pinged with a text, before I started the SUV I checked it. Seeing that it was Fiona I opened the message, *Going to bed. Alarm is set. This bed feels lonely without you.*

Texting back I said, *Be home soon.*

The woman sitting beside me was glaring daggers at me for which I had no fucking clue why.

Ignoring her I drove the three hours to unload her and the baby to Powers. I kept a vigil watch on my surroundings taking different routes to ensure that we weren't followed.

The woman asked all kinds of questions and to be honest it was no wonder the man had hurt her, I know that was wrong to think, but goddamn did she ever shut up?

She asked my full name, how old I was, what my favorite color was, why did I have so many tattoos, on and on. When she finally stopped talking after she got no response from me, the rest of the drive was easy.

The moment I pulled up at the cabin that Powers was using for this, I climbed out, nodded, then watched as the woman climbed out, and grabbed her baby. Grabbing her bag I handed it to Heathen who was standing beside him.

Just as I was walking away, she called out to me, "Hey Knox, why can't we go with you?"

"Not how this works. I know you were explained that." I told her.

However, I should have known that the glares the woman had been throwing at me as I walked away should have told me that I needed to be prepared for a woman that had felt scorned.

Jumping in the SUV I drove back home, sadly it was already eleven in the morning. Fiona was having her girl day. Texting her I said, *Clubhouse.*

I had just taken a sip of my whiskey when I felt her. Looking over at the door I let out a massive growl.

What the fuck? I felt my throat tighten when I took in what she had on, or more accurately what she didn't have on.

I was up and out of my chair so fast I knocked the chair backward.

The women around her turned their wide-eyed gazes to me as I plowed through the bodies to get to her.

Zeroing my focus in on her I glared as I looked up and down her body.

"Mine." I growled when I got close to her, wrapped an arm around her waist, hauled her to me, then kissed her.

Any other fuckers chose to go after her after this, then they would be meeting the end of my fist.

Pulling back I said, "Go change." I fingered the material, "Bedroom later."

She smirked, winked, then I saw the blinding smile that she tossed to the other women. Confusion marred my brow as I watched her, all of the ole' ladies, pull hundred dollar bills out of the tops of their dresses and handed them over to Fiona.

"The fuck is this shit." Cotton pointed to their actions.

"Well, dearest husband, we all had a bet, you see. We bet a hundred dollars to the woman whose man went caveman first. And Knox was the only one that reacted the moment we stepped through."

Cotton growled, "I was talking to someone."

"I was trying to figure out what I was seeing." Cooper muttered as he ran his hands over Miriam's body.

"You took my breath away baby." Walker told Sydney.

All of the women rolled their eyes as they too turned to follow Fiona.

"Thanks for making us look like assholes." Garret muttered darkly as he took off after Valerie.

With a straight face I muttered, "If the shoe fits."

I waited, four-point five seconds as all of them laughed. Smiling, I turned and walked off.

"Was that an actual fucking smile? I'm buying Fiona a beer." Shaking my head at Cotton I walked back over to where I was while I waited for Fiona to get finished, I needed her to tape up my hands.

The moment she made it to me, I nodded. Much fucking better.

"Have fun?" I asked her as we waited for York to start the night off.

"Love makes your soul crawl out from its hiding place." – Zora Neale Hurston

## Chapter 8

### Fiona

As we walked into the clubhouse for the Bare Knuckle No Holds Barred fight night I was giddy with laughter.

The women and I had a spa day while the men were setting things up. I have yet to see Knox since we woke up this morning, and all of us girls had hatched a plan so to speak. We each bought the raciest dress that we could find at this little boutique.

We wanted to see which man would turn into a caveman first. And I was then the proud owner of five hundred dollars.

I had just changed into some short cut-off jean shorts and a white racer back tank with a Chief Indian on the front of it in watercolors. I loved it.

The other ladies all dressed the same.

Grabbing a beer I made my way back out to the backyard, standing on my tip toes, I looked for Knox.

The moment my eyes landed on him I walked over to him.

As soon as I made it to him, he handed me some tape. "Hands?"

The moment I grabbed it he asked, "Have fun?"

I smiled as I showed him my manicure and my pedicure, "Better for scratches." He winked playfully; I loved this side of him.

Nodding he moved the chair beside him closer so I could sit down. The moment I had his hands taped up I looked in his eyes, "Don't get hurt. I'll beat someone's ass if you do."

"Sweetheart, have you looked at me?" I paused; the sweetheart thing was new.

"Yes but still," I warned him while I glared at him to make my point.

York came over the sound system, "Alright ladies and knuckleheads, the first round of fighting is about to start. Let's do this."

The moment we stood I walked with him to see who he would be up against first.

The name said West.

After Knox stepped in the ring, I walked over to the ladies, grabbed a beer, and stood with them.

When Knox bounced on the balls of his feet, I felt the adrenaline start to pump through my veins.

"He better not get hurt." I muttered.

"He won't. At least not with these puny assholes." Valerie smiled as she watched Garret stretch.

I turned my head as the other fighter stepped into the ring, and then with one powerful punch from Knox the other man fell. Out cold.

I cheered and whistled for all of the men, until Knox got in the ring with Garret.

And then I had to close my eyes and cringe at one of the punches that Garret handed him.

"Like your man Valerie, but he's about to get his ass kicked by me." I told her.

"That's…." then Knox landed one of his own. "Okay, Knox is getting the same thing from me."

Smiling, I turned just as Knox landed a kick to Garret's middle that sent him ass over tea kettle.

When Garret shook the move off, he tapped the mat three times.

When Knox was declared the winner, because Cotton didn't fight tonight, York stepped in the ring, "Now that you won, will you be challenging Cotton for his presidency?

Knox snarled, "Fuck no."

After everyone laughed, because it wasn't that Knox was scared of Cotton, it was that he respected the man too much.

Shots were poured and slug back.

While I stood there with the women, a group of men that hadn't signed up to fight walked over to us.

They didn't speak to the ole' ladies but one of them spoke to me.

"And who is this?" He wasn't ugly at all, had I seen him before Knox, well to be honest I didn't even want to think about that. The man had dark hair like Knox's and he had blue eyes that were handsome, however, he reminded me of Cole with his arrogance, and that just rubbed me the wrong way.

But before I could turn the man down, a dark shadow fell over us.

I knew Knox wouldn't say anything to the man. But then I was fucking floored.

"Mine." He growled as he stepped in front of me, placed his still wrapped hand around my waist and pulled me to his sweaty back.

"She don't have a kutte on." The man bowed his chest at Knox.

"Don't need one."

It was then that Cotton walked over. Yelling loudly he asked, "Who does Fiona belong to?"

Then a resounding "Knox" came from every direction.

That night after I had massaged his shoulders while we were in the claw foot bathtub, he leaned his head back on my shoulder.

"I thought claw foot bathtubs were small. I'm surprised we both fit."

"Had it custom made." I nodded.

"Can I ask you a question?" I asked him, this was something that I had thought about daily.

When he didn't reply I asked, "Why do you suppose my mother gave me away?"

I felt his body tense, "Don't know sweetheart. Hate to say this, but I'm glad. Wouldn't trade you for anything."

That night instead of being in control, we shared in the passion that was between us.

The next day I was sitting beside the ole' ladies when the front door opened. I looked up and saw a red-haired woman with a baby in her arms.

"Can we help you?" Garret called out to her.

"Yes." The woman walked further in the room.

I heard Knox mutter, "Dove."

Looking at him I saw that he was staring at Cotton who immediately jerked his head to stare at the woman, "Everyone but ole' ladies and brothers, get the fuck out."

As everyone was filing out, I grabbed my beer and stood then before I could take a step I heard, "Sweetheart?"

I looked at Knox, who then nodded at me to retake my seat. I looked at Cotton to see him nod as well. The moment I sat back down, the ole' ladies lifted their drinks and said, "Welcome to the family." Grinning, I clinked glasses with them, unsure of what that all meant.

Looking at Knox, he winked at me, and then his face closed down as he stared at the other woman.

"Now, what the fuck are you doing here?"

"It wasn't safe where I was taken, I saw my ex within a few hours. I've come here because I don't trust anyone other than him to protect me." She said as she pointed to Knox.

"What's a Dove?" I asked the other women quietly.

"Let Knox tell you." Novalie whispered out.

"Then did you go to the contact we told you?" Cotton asked her.

"No. I don't trust anyone else other than Knox." She continued on. "He and I had a connection." I heard her say smugly.

"Well way I see it, you have two options, we relocate you one more time, or you're out of our program."

"I'll pay. Fifty thousand dollars."

"We don't need your money. That isn't why we do this." Cotton continued on.

"Seventy-five for Knox to protect me." I heard Cooper cough to disguise his laughter.

"Look, you aren't listening to me. That isn't how we do things. That isn't how we operate." I could see Novalie out of the corner of my eye as she glared at the woman.

"Well I don't care. If you don't have Knox protect me, then I'll go to everyone and I'll ruin your little operation you have going on."

I saw Knox's nostrils flaring. Standing, I made my way over to him, the veins in his neck were popping out.

Uncaring in the least I sat down in his lap and wrapped my arms around his neck as I held him close.

I felt his body loosen the merest inch as he wrapped me in his strong arms, pulled me close and buried his face in my neck.

"You don't threaten me and mine, little girl, now you just lucked out on us protecting you. You're out."

"The connection that I shared with him; was unlike anything I have ever felt before." The woman was going to end up getting bitch slapped.

When Knox's entire body tightened I whispered in his ear, "Take me."

He pulled back; I could see the anger swirling in his dark eyes. Without a word, he stood as I wrapped my legs around him.

I faintly heard Walker tell the woman, "You may think you shared a connection with Knox but that woman in his arms, she's the only one that has a connection to him."

Smiling into his neck, I squealed as he took me into a room. I didn't have time to take anything in, no he lifted my skirt so it bunched around my hips, and then he slid his massive cock inside of me.

I moaned as my pussy stretched around him. When I put my hands to the wall he growled, "On me."

Smiling I placed my hands on his shoulders then I did what I have wanted to do I scraped my finger nails on his skin.

The feel of his hard body beneath my hands as I felt him hitting my g-spot was enough to bring my climax home.

I looked into his eyes as my legs quivered around his waist.

"My room." He nodded his head around us.

But before I could take everything in, Knox started to pound even harder into me, with one hand on my ass, and the other hand bracing himself on the wall.

When he bit his lip, my orgasm burst free. "Knox." I moaned.

Just minutes later, Knox followed suit.

Thirty minutes later as I was coming down the steps with Knox at my side it was to see a man storm into the clubhouse as he said angrily. "Shaina, what the fuck?"

She spun around and glared at Cotton, "You called him?"

"He told us something completely different than what you did. Told us he only wanted his baby."

"Well he can't have him." She said, angrily.

"I've got a court order. Been looking for you all this time." The man said as he held out his order.

That was when I had enough, marching over I grabbed the baby out of her arms, carried him over to his father, and then while the woman was bitching, I backhanded her across the face.

"Grow the fuck up. Quit using the baby, its pieces of shit like you, why men don't trust women." I snarled.

It was then that cops came to the clubhouse, it was one that knew what Wrath MC did. In the that thirty minutes we had been in his room, he had told me that they save women from abusive relationships and they relocate them with a new identity.

It was the custom bike work and the guns that helped cover the operation.

They arrested the woman for kidnapping the baby.

Since we had other clubs still here from last night, the party raged in full swing.

I had just grabbed Knox and me a beer and a glass of whiskey, on my way back to him it was to see another woman try to put her hands on him.

The rational part of my brain quit working when I did what I did next, stepping between them with my back to Knox I growled, "Mine."

Luckily, the woman didn't need more than that she stalked off.

Turning I looked up into his eyes. And then I felt my entire world fall apart around me.

Knox got in my face, I shrunk back. The snarl on his lips terrified me. Had I overstepped?

Hadn't he claimed me in front of that man and his club? What was different about what I had done?

Then he stormed out of the clubhouse, started his bike, and roared away.

Never mind that I had ridden here with him. I fought the tears that threatened to spill over.

All of the women looked at me with pitying glances.

I put the beer and the glass on the table, walked over to Phoebe and asked, "Can you take me home?"

"Yeah sweetie, come on." I didn't look at anyone as I kept my gaze on my feet as I walked out of the clubhouse.

"I've never been up here." Phoebe said in awe as we drove up the road to the house.

Sadly, I asked her, "Do you want a tour?"

"Think I'll wait sweetie, I know what Knox did was wrong, but he's the best, make his ass grovel."

Three hours later I was drunk on my ass as I stumbled to his bed and fell face first, crying into Kida's fur.

Knox had been gone for ten days, I hadn't bothered to call or text him. What I had done was packed my bags and if he didn't come home today, I was leaving.

"A man only becomes wise when he begins to calculate the approximate depth of his ignorance." – Gian Carlo Menotti

## Chapter 9

### Knox

I know that I left in a hurry. To be honest I wasn't sure what I was feeling. All of these feelings were abhorrent to me. I didn't rely on anyone. I had me. And when she claimed me, this disgusting piece of human trash, I had walked away from her. Pissed at my own fucking self, I drove for another hour clearing my head. I stopped at a stoplight, looked to my right, and saw a jewelry store.

However, I continued on, trying to calm the raging monster that stayed inside of me. Two hours later I knew that I had fucked up, I had been about to turn my bike around and head back to the clubhouse when my phone rang.

Hoping that it was Fiona, I growled when I saw that it was Cotton.

"Yeah."

Got a Dove. Relocate her. Sent the information to you." He hung up.

Fucking Christ.

The entire rescue had been fucked up beyond all proportions. I hadn't made it to the woman in time, but I had made it to the children just as their father put his finger on the trigger to kill the little boy. Over my dead body. Thankfully, an ally of ours had showed up, Zagan MC and we were able to get the two children relocated with a distant relative that had been trying to get the mother and the kids to come live with her.

In all the time I had been gone, Fiona hadn't texted nor called, I knew that I had fucked up, and if I didn't fix this and soon, I'd lose the best damn thing that ever happened to me.

Ten days. That has been the longest that I have ever been away from her. If someone would have told me fifteen years ago that one mere slip of a woman would be able to ease the raging monster that I felt in me every day of my life, I would have ended them. No questions asked.

Just the sound of her voice ceased all of the voices that I heard on a day-to-day basis. Voices of the lives that I had taken. The cries from those pleading with me to not inflict pain on them. The whispers from my childhood. The ones where people would say that I was nothing more than my mother's whore. To be used when it benefitted her. To be used when she needed her dealer to give her, her next escape. That the dealer only wanted little boys when you couldn't pay.

Sadly, those whispers had been true.

Now, when she smiles, that one single action causes all of the darkness that swarms around me to brighten, almost to the point where I feel like a kid before my carefree life literally ended.

The feel of her hands on my body, now that, that is the best thing of all. Her touch erases away all of the dark, sick, twisted things that I have had done to me.

From the time I was four until I turned seven.

Why did those things end when I turned seven? Why was I in juvenile detention until I turned seventeen? Why hadn't I been tried as an adult for murdering my mother by smothering her with a pillow? Why hadn't I been given a far lengthier term for killing the sadistic son of a bitch?

Simple. Because no one knew about what I had done to my mother. Her death had been ruled a suicide, an overdose. The only crime I had admitted to was killing that man. I never spoke about what she had allowed to happen to me. I never spoke about the times that she herself locked my bedroom door after she allowed that man inside of my room.

Shaking those thoughts from my head as I drove home, I stopped at that same stop light and looked left. There was that jewelry store.

Since no one was behind me, I moved to the turning lane.

Walking into the jewelry store had a cold sweat hitting my body, I almost turned around and left, however, the idea of making Fiona mine permanently, of giving all of me to her didn't scare me anymore.

Two hours later I walked out with my purchases.

The moment I pulled up on my bike at the clubhouse, I saw Fiona's car in the lot.

Everyone was outside since I had texted Cotton that I was almost there. I had to stop to see Clutch, I had another crow added to my arm. That man would never harm those children again.

So I ignored the insistence in my president's voice. I ignored the bodies that surrounded me, trying to stop me, that was a fucking joke.

I plowed through the bodies until I saw her.

She was sitting with her back to the door surrounded by the ole' ladies.

Almost as if she knew I was coming for her, she turned her head, the moment our eyes locked I saw hurt in them, standing there in the open-door way for all to hear, I told her, "I'm sorry. I'm yours if you'll have me."

Fiona stared at me, then I saw her she was up and out of her chair so fast that it seemed gravity didn't apply to her.

When she reached me she threw herself at me, I caught her in my arms as I hauled her up my body.

I knew that I was holding her too tight, but she didn't say a word, no she merely ran her hands along the back of my neck while whispering so only I could hear, "I'm right here honey."

We stood there in the doorway while my brothers walked back in, setting her down on her feet, I looked in her eyes. Knew that I would be groveling on my knees begging her for her forgiveness.

"I know I overstepped and I'm sorry for that, and…" I put my finger over her lips to stop her.

There was nothing that she did wrong.

"Love makes your soul crawl out from its hiding place." – Zora Neale Hurston

## Chapter 10

### Fiona

With his fingers underneath my chin, he lifted my face to look at him, "Education, sweetheart, the only woman for me is you."

I stared into his eyes as I tentatively placed my hand over his heart, waiting for him to lean away from my touch since we were in front of other people, only he didn't, no, he leaned forward.

The moment my hand touched his chest, I broke.

Tears fell out of my eyes as he wrapped those arms around me and hauled me into his chest. This, this was where I was meant to be.

"You ever walk away from me again; you better be prepared to grovel." I said with my face buried in his chest.

Knox then stunned me, as I felt the rumble of his laughter.

"Done sweetheart." I pulled away from him, looked up into his eyes as he wiped the tears away and then ever so gently, he bent his head as he kissed me ever so carefully.

Taking a breath I wanted to test out this change in him, "Dance with me?"

His smile was breathtaking, he offered me his hand as he led me onto the dance floor.

With his arms around me, I lifted my hands and grabbed ahold of his biceps, "So does this mean I can touch you whenever I want?"

"What do you think?" Grinning, I moved my hands from his biceps to his chest.

I melted when Knox started to sing softly along with the music that was coming through the speakers, "You're as smooth as Tennessee whiskey. You're as sweet as strawberry wine". Not wanting him to be in this moment alone, I sang back to him, "You're as warm as a glass of brandy, and I stay stoned on your love all the time."

After we danced I went into the kitchen to help Novalie and Lucy clean up. Just as I had turned off the water from washing my hands I heard. "He lets you touch him?" Amberly asked.

I know that she is in love with him, but I answered her honestly as I grabbed a towel and dried my hands, "Yes."

"Umm, how long have you known him?"

"Four years."

Her eyes widened. "So it's been you. He would sit in the corner of a room with a glass of whiskey and just stare off into space."

Seeing that this woman obviously cared a great deal about Knox, I opened up to her and admitted something that ate me up every single day, "I know what you're thinking. That I don't deserve him. And you're right, I really don't. I shouldn't have been a fool and stayed with my ex when the man of my dreams was literally standing right in front of me."

"Good you saw that. He's easy to love." She said. I nodded at her. And then she left the room.

Two days later when I hadn't seen her at the clubhouse Novalie told me that Amberly had packed up her things and left. I had felt awful for that but she had assured me that Knox only ever had eyes for me.

Later that day I laughed as Kida ran around the backyard enjoying the colder weather. When Knox threw a stick for him, he lunged off his back legs, jumped in the air and caught it.

I melted when I looked at Knox as he tossed me a wink. Then the resounded whack of the axe that he was wielding sounded as he cut up another log for firewood.

I felt it deep. Watching his shirt straining as it tried to contain his muscles.

With the last stack of firewood that Knox had split, I carried it inside and set it in the wood box that he had beside the fireplace.

"I'm going to go jump in the shower." I told him as I headed to the bathroom.

As I was in the shower, the power went out. Do you know how weird it is to condition your hair in the dark? Surprisingly, thanks to muscle memory, it isn't that hard.

Just as I turned the water off, I noticed there was a little light in the bathroom.

Smiling, I opened the shower door and saw a candle that was sitting beside a stack of towels that I hadn't placed there.

Tip-toeing on the cold tile floor I reached for them and was shocked to find that they were warm. Only Knox would think of this.

I shrugged into one of them and sighed at the warmth that wrapped around me.

After I dried off, I walked into the bedroom to see a pair of his knee-high wool socks, a pair of pajama pants and my comfy off-the-shoulder light pink sweater.

Putting them all on I grinned, how had I gotten this lucky?

Walking out of the bedroom I heard old soft rock playing on my record player.

As I rounded the corner out of the hall I stopped to look at my man.

He was sitting in a chair with his massive forearms on the tops of his knees watching as the fire crackled.

The moment he saw me, he turned, grabbed a pillow, and placed it on the floor in between his legs.

"Come." I looked at him and saw that he was nodding between his legs. "Back to me."

Smiling a small smile I made my way over to him and sat down on the pillow that he had there. And then color me surprised, Knox had my comb in his hand and he started working out the tangles in my hair.

After he finished with the tangles, my big man braided my hair, he had watched me every time I braided my hair. I leaned my head back into Knox's chest, and marveled at how much things had changed between Knox and me.

Getting to touch him, getting to have these little moments with Knox, these were the moments that I lived for.

Looking out through the window I saw that the snow was raging on.

I snuggled further into his chest as Kida wrapped his warm body around my legs.

It was later on in the night while we were lying in bed with three candles lighting the room that I found myself wanting to give him something back. Something that I wanted as well. But I also knew that all of the times that he had been inside of me, he had been holding back. Holding back from what I wasn't sure, but I wanted to know.

"Tell me what you need, Knox. Don't be afraid. Give me all of you." I had no idea what I was asking.

What I did know was that I wanted all of this man, every single molecule of him. All of the darkest parts of him.

His eyes that I had fallen in love with turned almost black as he looked down at me.

"You don't know what you're asking. You're the last person on this god-forsaken planet that I would ever harm." He said gravely.

"Knox, please. I won't break." I muttered into the darkness.

I saw the indecision in his dark eyes and then after a few minutes, he nodded.

I almost pouted when he got up from the bed, only to return a few moments later with some rope and a knife.

I laid there anticipating what he was about to do. I watched in avid fascination as he brought the knife to his mouth and held it with his teeth.

"You're sure about this? Once we do this, there is no escaping me Fi. I'll follow you to the ends of the earth. You. Are. Mine." he growled.

I nodded. I wasn't afraid of this man; I wasn't sure how I knew that but I did. "I'm sure Knox."

Instead of responding, he grabbed my right wrist then my left as he straddled me with his knees on either side of me.

I felt the rope being tied around my wrists to the bedposts. It wasn't painful, but it was tight enough that I couldn't move my wrists.

Once he had done that he braced his hands on the bed posts looking down at me. "Safe word. Crimson."

I looked up at him and without saying a word I allowed my gaze to communicate into his eyes of how sure I was about this.

As he trailed the thin blade along my skin, goosebumps pebbled, at the site of them Knox lifted his head, there, in those dark orbs I saw something. Something I have never seen before.

Was this the man that he showed the enemy? Was this the man that everyone feared?

But then when the tip of the knife cut into a part of my inner thigh, instead of feeling pain, I felt pleasure.

"What is our safe word?" he rasped.

"Crimson." I breathed out.

"Good girl."

When he knelt his head, licking off the small trickle of blood from the inside of my thigh I almost came right then and there. The pleasure had enfolded all around my body, I wanted, no I needed to touch him, but then his words stopped me, *'you touch me and I'll quit'*, no, that was the last thing that I wanted him to do.

I wanted more.

The more I needed, I didn't know, it wasn't until he came up my body, the moment he nibbled on my bottom lip, caressing it with his tongue, then when his tongue entered my waiting mouth I moaned.

The taste of my blood on his tongue was intoxicating.

I've never felt that before.

Was that something that I had been missing?

Had he seen that unveiled part of me on the day we met? Perhaps.

He trailed the tip of the blade between my breasts after he had pulled each nipple into his mouth, suckled on them, then and only then when he was apparently satisfied with his work, he trailed the blade down to my belly as he sat it aside to bury his tongue in my pussy.

My back arched as his tongue licked me from bottom to top, parting my labia and then he finally brought his tongue to my clit.

I moaned, wanting to touch him, wanting to hold on to him, to trail my fingernails all over his heated skin.

I heard a warning in his gravelly tone as he said, "Don't come sweetheart."

"Knox..." I groaned.

I would want him to try not to come if the roles were reversed.

Then he gave me what I had been craving, like a shot, he lifted, then he entered me in one brutal shove. Filling me. I felt his hard length start to move in and out of me.

Looking up into his eyes I was breathing hard as I was trying to hold my orgasm back, "Knox..."

"Not yet sweetheart." He warned yet again.

Growling low in my throat as he hit my g-spot, I saw him smirk, laughing I called out, "Knox, please..."

With three more strokes I heard the words I had been waiting for, "Come."

And I came. Hard. I also felt him still as he climaxed as well with a growl that was so intense even I shook from it.

After he had come down, he reached up, untied my hands and then he gathered me in his arms.

With my head on his chest I knew that there was nowhere else I wanted to be.

If I knew that he would be ready to hear those three words that were made up of 8 letters I would be screaming them from the tops of my lungs.

She is both hellfire and holy water.

And the flavor you taste depends on how you treat her.

-Sneha Pal

# Chapter 11

## Knox

With my hands against the wall on either side of her head, I asked, "How did you know?"

"Know what?" she looked at me with an impish grin.

"That I needed you in my life. You looked past the dark, down into the deepest part of my soul, a soul that I had lost when I was four." I wasn't afraid of letting her see this part of me, this part that was broken, shattered, demolished unless she was near me.

How could one person rely on another human being so much?

"Knox, I don't see a man that has been hurt. I don't see a man that has demons. What I see is a man that I would walk through the fiery gates of hell to bring back to me. A man that holds me when I cry. Who surprises me with breakfast in the mornings. Who walks against traffic so that if a car gets out of control, they have to go through you to get to me. I see a man that I want to live an eternity with. But most importantly I see a man that I love with all of my heart."

I took in everything she had said, but that little four-letter word had the power to completely undo me.

She knew that she would never hear those words from me, but just knowing that she wasn't afraid to let her feelings be known, I knew that I didn't deserve her. But I was a selfish asshole that way.

So I was going to keep on taking everything she had to give me.

Deciding that now was a good time, I reached inside my kutte pocket and pulled out a small jewelry bag.

Handing it to her I watched as her eyes widened.

She opened it carefully and the moment she pulled out a delicate white gold chain that was attached to a white gold dandelion, she stared at it, I saw tears hit her cheeks.

Lifting a finger, I wiped them away.

"Like it?"

"Knox, I don't know what to say. Thank you. I freaking love it, will you put it on me?"

I grabbed the delicate chain in my hands as I fumbled to get the clasp.

The moment I had it connected, I leaned over her as I watched it settle between her collarbones.

"It's freaking beautiful thank you." But that wasn't the only way she thanked me, no she dropped to her knees right there in our bedroom as she gave me a blowjob.

Rolling over in bed I opened my eyes, expecting to see Fiona there. When I didn't see her, I rolled out of bed, pulled on some work out pants, then I walked through the house looking for her.

I looked out the front window and saw her on the porch swing, pushing it off with her bare foot that was attached to her bare leg that led straight to my heaven.

After I made it to the open-door way, seeing her in my flannel caused the caveman in me to growl.

She turned her head as her entire face softened. "There's coffee in the pot."

Instead of going back inside I walked over to her, wrapped my hand in her hair, tilting her head back I brought my mouth down on hers.

When I pulled away I said, "Morning sweetheart."

"Morning honey." Then I placed a kiss on the top of her nose, only then did I grab myself a cup of coffee and joined her on the front porch swing.

Kida was laying in the front yard sunbathing, enjoying this cooler weather we had.

The moment I sat down I asked, "What's your question of the day?" Here lately she has been asking me random questions

"What's your middle name?"

I sighed, "My mother didn't think enough of me to give me one." That had always rubbed me the wrong way.

"Can I give you one?" She asked me in a giddy tone.

With a brow raised I asked her, "You want to?"

"Umm yeah, that would be freaking cool." The excitement in her voice was why I was agreeing to do this.

"Okay, what is it?"

"Drumroll please?" And like the sap I am for her, I drum rolled out a beat. Her smile was payment enough.

"Knox Stephen McCord." That was pretty good, had a good ring to it at least.

"Why Stephen?" I asked her, of all the names she could come up with, what was the reason behind that particular one?

"It's the middle name of one of my all-time favorite bands, the lead singers to be exact."

"And which band is this?"

The name of a band that I never expected her to say, came out of her mouth, "Shinedown."

"I like it. I'll add it to my shit." She leaned her head over and laid it on my shoulder.

I had found myself smiling even more the longer I was in her presence. Heaven help the bastard that ever dared to take her from me. Because the devil would be the least of his worries.

My phone pinged with a text, I grabbed it out of my pocket as I looked at the screen.

"Party tonight." I said aloud as she squealed, jumped up and ran to the bedroom to get ready.

Tossing my head back I laughed.

I sat on my barstool as my woman danced with her hands up in the air, always one to enjoy the moment, I had to growl at some dumb fucks that thought it was okay to approach her.

Thankfully, my growl had been loud enough to make them take a giant as fuck step back.

After she danced some more with the girls, she walked off the makeshift dance floor as she made her way to me.

I tagged her a bottle of water, opening it, and handed it to her when she reached me, "Drink."

She winked, "Yes sir. Bossy pants."

After she finished with her water she leaned into me to whisper, "Tell me something, what is your darkest fantasy?"

This woman was everything to me. There was nothing I wouldn't do for her, and if it included getting her body undermine, then I was all for it.

Pulling away from her I sat there with her leaning into my body, looking into her eyes, I saw that she wasn't drunk at all, no far from it.

"Trust?"

"With everything."

Nodding, I grabbed her hand and pulled her through the masses out the back of the clubhouse.

The moment we made it to my shed I stopped as I looked down at her.

"Fi…." I was cut off when she threw my words at me.

"Knox. Give me you." She said and that was what she was going to get.

With her hand still in mine I pulled her into the shed, bolted the door.

Walking in the darkness I flipped on the light switch.

Her sudden gasp at everything in here almost had me ending this entire fucking thing.

That was until she turned to face me. What I saw in those eyes was unlike anything I have ever seen.

Grabbing my phone, I pulled up a playlist for when I worked out.

"Strip." Emotion was clogging up my throat.

I stood there as I watched her taking off her clothes, when she got to a certain chord she started to dance.

The moment she stepped out of her skirt I ordered, "Stop. Leave your heels on."

She froze as she looked at me.

Grabbing my knife I walked over to her, with the sharp side facing me I slid it in her panties, never once breaking eye contact with her, then I flicked my wrist, slicing her panties.

When they fell down I grabbed her hand, pulled her over to the end of the table.

"Hands." When she placed them on the table, I placed each wrist in a cuff.

"Still trust me?"

Her face softened as she said, "Always."

I grabbed a whip from my wall. Walked back over to her as I shrugged out of my kutte and t-shirt. Then I took off my boots, jeans, and my boxer briefs.

I brought the whip down on her ass lightly.

She hissed out with a moan.

"My sweetheart likes that?"

"Do the other." She didn't have to ask me a second time.

The moment I brought the whip down on her other cheek, she moaned yet again.

I ran the whip down her spine, then grinned when the goosebumps pebbled up on her flesh.

"Knox, please…"

I reached for my pocket, only to find out that I didn't have a condom, I stilled.

"Knox.."

"We can't we'll have to finish this when we get to my room." My throbbing cock was angry with me.

"Why?"

"No condom."

"Knox, please, I trust you." She wiggled her ass.

"I'll pull out." I swallowed hard, and then I fingered her clit, shocked to discover that she was already wet.

For the first time in my life I entered a body without a condom on, son of a fucking bitch.

As I was pounding into her from behind, I leaned forward and bit her shoulder. I wanted her to always wear my mark. For others to see that she was mine.

Once I bit down hard, I drew blood. Her moan called to some part of me, I couldn't help but lick the puncture marks.

Grabbing a fist full of her black hair I jerked her head back, "You like that. You like wearing my mark?"

"Yes Knox." I kissed her hard, teeth clashing, tongues invading each other's mouths.

Thrusting into her with my hand still wrapped in her hair I pounded even harder into her.

So hard in fact that the metal slab was even shaking with my thrusts.

"Knox, I'm close." She moaned, but I wasn't through.

I had one more thing to do. With my hand on her throat I squeezed, just enough pressure to feel her pulse beat even faster.

With every breath she took a moan escaped her.

"Don't come Fi."

"Knox." She moaned which caused my dick to jump.

It was then that we heard two women talking outside of the shed. "I swear that man." I didn't stop pounding into her.

"I know, I mean, I came tonight to try and get in that man's bed." One woman said rather nasally,

"I told you to give it up. He never looks or talks to anyone."

And then Fiona's back arched, her pussy squeezed hard, and I came right along with her the moment I felt my spine tingle.

"I even bought this outfit. I mean god. And that woman that was with him. I'm prettier than her. I mean she wore a long skirt and a form-fitted top? To a biker clubhouse?" I growled when I realized they were talking about my woman.

"They got nothing on you." I took the cuffs off of her wrists, growling at myself for how red they were.

Seeing Fiona like that, any other time, would have my blood boiling. Seeing someone do that to her.

I was a son of a bitch.

As we cleaned up, the two girls were still chattering. I looked down at my woman and saw a tinkle in her eyes.

We grabbed baby wipes that I used on certain things to clean up ourselves.

Once everything was back in place and we were both dressed we walked to the door hand in hand.

However what I thought she was going to say when we emerged from the shed wasn't what came out of her mouth.

The moment I unbolted the door, the two women stopped talking as they froze.

"He happens to think I'm sexier when I walk out of the bedroom in a pair of his knee-length socks and a huge sweatshirt." Fiona simply grinned at them as we walked by.

"Oh and the reason why you didn't get in his bed, is because he was waiting for me." She tossed over her shoulder.

It ate at me the entire drive home until I had her in my arms as I carried her in the house when she muttered three words drowsily, "Love you honey."

How could she love me after what I had just done to her?

Whatever it was, I wasn't going to question it. I was going to grab hold of those words and live every day to earn them.

"Some men have thousands of reasons why they cannot do what they want to, when all they need is one reason why they can." – Martha Graham

## Chapter 12

### Fiona

Yesterday…. I had no words. When I awoke this morning I was sore in places that I hadn't even known could be sore.

However, on my nightstand, there had been a little note.

*'I know your sore, I've already gotten your bath water ready, go soak in it and enjoy a mimosa.'*

*-Knox.*

When I had read that note, I had ran for the bathroom, still naked as the day I was born, and there, sitting on the vanity was a mimosa in a champagne flute. I had to pinch myself to make sure that this really was my life. That I really was with this man, one who didn't give any part of himself to anyone, but me.

So there I was fifteen minutes later, my glass of orange juice with champagne was halfway demolished when I looked up as the door opened. There stood my man.

"Soon as you get done taking you for a ride. Bike rally for kids with down syndrome" Smiling I nodded.

Finishing with my bath after he left, I dried off, and dressed in jeans and a long-sleeved shirt with my boots.

As soon as I walked down the hall the smell of bacon filled my senses.

The moment I turned the corner I saw Knox standing at the stove.

He turned his head to look at me. And I almost melted on the spot. "Feel better?" I looked at him and nodded.

And then I did something that I have been wanting to do, I walked up behind him and wrapped my arms around his waist, leaned into him, and placed a kiss between his shoulder blades.

After we ate breakfast we mounted the bike. We may have made a pit stop to the bedroom so I could thank him properly.

Traveling down I-85 the wind whipping at my hair, this was where I wanted to be. To have this feeling of freedom every single second of every single day.

Although, I knew that this freedom that I was feeling wasn't just because I was on a bike going eighty-five miles an hour, no, it was all due to the man that I had my arms wrapped around. The man that had muscles on top of muscles. This feeling was all thanks to Knox.

What had made this feeling even better was when Knox brought his massive hand down to my calf as he ran his hand up my calf then along my thigh and back down where it rested on my calf.

I had heard the other ole' ladies talking about this feeling, but I have never felt it, not until now. The power of the leg grab.

They said that this showed that the man in front of you considered you his in every way imaginable.

I knew that I wasn't going to get more from Knox, that just wasn't him. He wanted to be free. He wanted to be able to take off when he wanted.

And truthfully, I would love to have his last name. I would love to carry his children.

However, that saying, I would have rather loved what I had than to have never loved at all was one hundred percent true.

The events from yesterday had me wanting to do it again.

As we pulled into formation with the rest of the MC we headed to a bike rally.

I smiled as we pulled up beside Walker and Sydney, thankfully, the women had all planned to wear the same color shirts, royal blue.

We traveled for another hour, and in that time more bikes joined in, it was one massive convoy. Cars and trucks had pulled over at intersections to make sure we had all gotten through.

Society as a whole wasn't as demolished as one would think.

The moment we arrived at the location, there were bikes on top of bikes. I was glad to be a part of something like this.

Smiling at a young girl that was manning a booth where they sold engraved leather cuffs, I walked over to her..

"These are amazing."

"Thank you. My dad does the artwork and I'm the face of the brand."

"Wow, that's awesome." I picked up two cuffs as I examined them, they were a matching pair. The cuffs were dark leather, and they each had a crow in flight on them.

"I'll take these two." I smiled as I handed them to her.

"Don't you want to know how much they cost?"

"Do the proceeds benefit this rally?"

"Yes, fifty percent of each sale."

"Okay."

Her smile got even wider as she told me my total. I could see why she was a little hesitant but for this cause they were worth it. Besides, they were engraved by hand. You could see minor mistakes that told me they weren't done by a machine.

"That'll be sixty dollars." She said with a bright smile.

I grabbed my cash and pulled out three twenties. Handing them to her, she put them in a little money bag, "Do you want me to wrap them in tissue paper for you?"

"Sure, that would be great."

Phoebe walked over, bumped my shoulder then asked, "What did you get?"

"Two cuffs that have crows on them."

Her eyes brightened as she too took in the cuffs, and that was how ten minutes later every ole' lady of Wrath MC bought two cuffs each.

The girl was stunned speechless and when her dad walked over, he stopped when most of his cuffs had been purchased.

"I don't... I don't know what to say."

"Do you have a website? I'm sure we would like to buy more later on as well."

'We do. Umm... here's my card. It has my website on it." He then handed all of us cards.

The two of them hugged excitedly as we left and I couldn't help the smile that broke out on my face along with the other ladies.

"This can't be fuckin good. All of y'all are smiling fucking wide." Xavier said as we came upon them looking at a bike that was up for auction.

"We just made someone's day I think. Felt good." Phoebe told them.

York lifted a brow, "How did y'all do that?"

"Well when we saw Phoebe looking at something because Fiona had gone over there first to buy something we all followed and we all bought something." Marley smiled.

"What?" Knox asked me.

Grinning, I opened the bag, then pulled out the tissue paper, and showed him the two leather cuffs.

"Those are badass." He said as he grabbed them and checked them out, then he lifted his head to look at me, "What are these for?"

"Well I figured I would use them as best friend bracelets."

"Yeah," His eyes narrowed, "And who is this best friend?" While I couldn't help but tease him, the other women showed their men what they got too.

"He's tall, built like nothing I have ever seen before. He has these eyes that just make me melt every time I look in them, and he happens to rock my world."

Grinning, he shook his head as he grabbed my right wrist, put one cuff on it, then he held out his wrist for me to do the same for his.

"Good. Not in a killing mood today." I tossed my head back and laughed.

I had just stepped out of the bathroom when I saw Cotton was standing there, thinking he was there for Novalie, I started to walk past him until he called my name, "Fiona?"

I stopped, turned my head to see him walk over to me.

"Look, that first night you came to the clubhouse, I know what I said caused you not to come back. I meant what I said, but I shouldn't have said it. Never seen my brother like this. I don't know everything he went through when he was a boy, but I think you know, and the fact that he trusted you says it all. Anyway, I just wanted to apologize."

"Thanks Cotton. And thank you for caring about him enough to say that to me. I would've done the same thing."

We were talking back and forth as we walked over to the group where they were standing in line to get some barbeque.

When I made it to Knox, it was to see his eyes were on Cotton, he looked down at me and asked, "Okay?"

"Yeah, he apologized for what he said that night in the clubhouse."

"Good. I respect him, but I won't hesitate to bring him a world of hurt."

Wrapping my arms around him I snuggled closer into his chest.

After I ordered for both of us, we chowed down.

We all ended up buying shirts that said, *I'm With Down*. They were royal blue with yellow lettering.

After the rally was over we all headed home, Knox and I had peeled off to hit the store.

While I walked beside Knox as he pushed a cart for a few things that we needed, we headed to the movies.

It took us about thirty minutes to browse everything for a little date night at the house.

Knox had growled eleven times at men that didn't know how to keep their eyes off of me. While I had to glare at quite a few women.

I buried my face in his neck, I was on pins and needles while we watched this movie. Why had I chosen it? The cover looked crazy; I was glad I hadn't eaten before a line had cut everyone except a little girl in half.

Later that night, I was about to order some birth control. "What are you doing?"

I looked at him as he was rubbing Kida's belly on our bed, "Ordering some birth control."

His eyebrow rose, "Why?"

"So that we don't have a baby unplanned." I didn't want any child to ever think that it wasn't wanted.

"Do you not want kids?" I froze as I was about to hit the order button.

"Yes I want them. I want at least three." While I looked in his eyes he shocked the hell out of me.

"Then why you ordering birth control?"

"We haven't really discussed it. I mean, are you ready to be a father?"

"I am if you're ready to be a mother. It's your call sweetheart. I'm for whatever you want."

And that was how I canceled my order, "I am."

"Okay. Suppose we practice making one right now?"

"How did I get so lucky to have you in my life?"

122

"Sweetheart, I'm the fucking lucky one."

And just like that we slipped from a serious conversation to making love.

"There are two ways of spreading light: to be the candle or the mirror that reflects it." – Edith Wharton

## Chapter 13

### Knox

While we were laying on bed that night after watching the movie with her head on my bicep I said, "You never talk about your pseudo grandparents since they went on that cruise for Thanksgiving. What happened?"

"Well if you can believe, they stepped off port at one of the islands, and they retired there. I mean they had already retired and everything, but they sold the house they had here and they moved there. They send an email every once and a while but according to them they are living their best life."

"Great for them. Shitty for you." I told her.

"I know. I mean when they took me and Sorcha in it was a relief. We shared a room there but I got new clothes every six months at least. Brand new ones with tags on them. I didn't have to move from there and throw my belongings in a trash bag. The first shower I had there, was the first time I got to use hot water."

"Damn babe. Never gonna bitch if you use all the hot water ever again."

She chuckled, "Damn straight."

I hadn't broached this subject with her but it was something I have always wanted to know, "Got another question for you?"

"What's that?"

"Have you ever tried to find your parents?" I felt her body tense.

She sat there, so still I wondered if she was ever going to answer me, but then she did, "I thought about it, yes. Just to ask them, why? Why did they have me and give me away? Thought about hiring a private detective but all I have is a note and a blanket. My birthday was determined to the directors of the orphanage to the best of their abilities. But even then, it would be difficult. Thought about doing that ancestry kit thing you see on television, maybe someone out there shares DNA with me and I can find a relative. Something."

"Whenever you're ready, let's do the ancestry thing. Yeah?"

I felt her smile on my skin before she replied, "Yeah."

"You got any questions?" I asked her.

"Yeah, will you agree to do it with me and see if we can find your dad?"

"If it's something you want me to do, then yeah babe."

"I don't want it to be because of me. I never want you to do something you don't won't to do ever. And I…" I cut her off when I placed my finger over her mouth.

"Sweetheart, don't think for one minute that anything you want me to do, that I won't want it as well."

After that we settled in deeper and within minutes of her body relaxing, my body relaxed and I fell asleep while I held the most important thing in my life, in my arms.

The next night we were all sitting around the fire pit with Kida lying at her feet.

Unable to help myself I chuckled as Fiona tossed every single lemon Skittle into the fire pit.

"What did the yellow one's ever do to you?" Walker asked her.

"They make me bitter." She said with a soft laugh.

"I don't like the green ones; they just taste off to me." Novalie chimed in.

"Okay, I'm the odd ball out, I hate Skittles, give me M&Ms any day of the week but they have to be the peanut ones." Lucy chimed in.

Which then caused the kids that were having s'mores to throw marshmallows at her.

"Hey, are y'all coming over to my parents' house for Sunday dinner tomorrow night?" Phoebe asked while she held Pebbles in her lap with Bash sitting on Xavier's lap.

I looked at Fiona to see her looking at me, "Okay?"

I saw her bite her bottom lip, and then she nodded. Looking at Phoebe I nodded.

The next afternoon, Fiona had changed three times, wanting to make a good first impression, after she put the first outfit on. Crazy woman.

"Car babe. Too fucking cold for you on the bike."

"Knox, I won't freeze." She grumbled as she pulled on her coat.

"Don't care." Huffing, she stomped out of the house. She was the only one that ever gave me as good as I got.

Opening her door for her I silently berated myself for my predicament. I wasn't a small man and trying to fit inside of her tiny ass tin can of a car was going to be painful.

I had bumped my knees thirteen times, yes I had counted. After we were done eating tonight, my ass was walking home. Fuck that.

"Are you sure they won't mind that I am here with you?" This was the third time she had asked me that.

"Fi…" I had to bite down the forcefulness of my growl.

"Knox, I'm a complete stranger to them." Instead of opening the car door, I pulled her across the console to sit in my lap even though it was a tight fit. I would be remedying this shit soon.

"Sweetheart, they took me in made me a part of their family. You're my family. They will love you just as I do."

Sitting there on my lap she finally nodded and then she said, "Okay. Let's do this."

Grinning, I squeezed her hip, then watched as she climbed out of my lap, thankfully she was a tiny thing so moving through the car wasn't hard to do for her. She was perfect for me.

As soon as I stepped out of the car I stretched, thank fuck that it had been a short drive. Scanning the area I rounded the hood of the car and opened her door for her.

"Thank you, Knox." Grinning down at her I nodded.

Hand in hand we walked up the front-drive.

As soon as we were about to knock on the door, it opened and there stood Phoebe. "Hey," when she smiled I knew that she had been watching us.

"Hey Phoebe, I wasn't sure if I needed to bring something because I forgot to ask you."

"Now that's what I like to hear, Knox, you found a good one. And no, we have plenty of food, I promise you." I looked at Sienna and then over her shoulder at Sean.

Smiling, Phoebe introduced Fiona, "Fiona this is my mom and dad, Sienna and Sean."

"It's very nice to meet you. You have a beautiful home."

"Well, if the women would move out of your way, you could see more of it." Sean laughed when Sienna and Phoebe immediately stepped aside.

"Forgive them their manners, welcome to our home dear." I reached out and shook Sean's hand.

Taking off my coat and Fiona's I hung them up by the door.

"Uncle Knox. Aunt Fiona!" Bash and Pebbles called out when we stepped into the living room.

"Hey guys, what are y'all playing?"

"Legos. Gramma and Grandpa bought us a new set." Bash said proudly.

"That's so cool." She looked at Sienna, "Do you need any help in the kitchen?"

"Actually everything is almost ready. Phoebe, can you set the table?"

Fiona nodded, then she sat down on the floor while she helped them work on the Lego set.

Xavier walked over and handed me a beer and Fiona a glass of sweet tea,

After a few minutes Sienna called everyone to the dining table to eat.

I had just passed the mashed potatoes to Fiona when Sienna asked, "So Fiona, Phoebe tells me that you work at Virginia's? I love that woman."

"Yes, Virginia has been a godsend to me." She told her.

I felt pride swell in my chest at my woman. She was trying. I know that this was all something that she had no experience with.

"Is Randy still cooking?" Sienna

"Yes and grumbling about the orders he has to fix. A few years ago, we had a customer and he sent his food back because things were touching. Then when Randy fixed that, he sent it back because the bacon was too crispy."

"Reminds me when Sienna was pregnant with Phoebe. If one thing wasn't right, she would send the plate back and refuse to eat it even if they fixed it."

Gone was the uncertainty in her voice as she laughed and chatted with Phoebe's parents.

"We are having a potluck next Sunday. So Fiona if you wouldn't mind, can you bring a side and possibly a dessert?"

"Banana pudding for dessert, okay?" I know how good that is, she made it a few weeks ago. I may or may not have eaten most of it while we watched a new show that she had been wanting to see.

Sienna smiled, "Perfect."

After we helped clean up, I took us home. No, I didn't walk. I was to fucking full to walk home.

While Fiona showered, and changed, I let Kida out, then I did the same, it wasn't until we were lying in bed that she said, "I'm really glad I went, I had a blast. So going to talk to Randy tomorrow and tease him."

When Fiona fell asleep, I grabbed my cell and looked at what I was going to be getting her tomorrow.

After I found what I was looking for, I turned off the light, rolled over, and wrapped my body around hers.

She snuggled closer in her sleep and sighed blissfully.

Thankfully while she'd been at work the next morning I had made a new purchase.

When Fiona's car came up the drive, she parked it between my bike and the newest addition that I had bought.

I smiled as I mentally prepared myself for the argument that was about to take place.

"Cherish the music that stirs in your heart." – Napoleon Hill

## Chapter 14

### Fiona

"Knox this is too much, I can't accept this." No one has ever done something like this for me. Normally, this would have been a major red flag for me, but with Knox, I knew that it wasn't.

"Fiona," he growled.

"Knox. I'm not with you because of what you can give me. I'll get a better car when I can afford it." I growled back.

"Well, I can't fit in your little car. What if something happens to my truck and my bike and we have to be somewhere?" There he went again with his logic.

"Well… I…" I didn't have a comeback for that one.

"Also, if you get hit, your car will be totaled. Doesn't matter where you get hit. And if the son of a bitch doesn't die before I get to you to make sure you're alright, then I'll kill them."

"Knox…."

"I'm not joking Fiona." And that was the truth, I knew that he wasn't.

Then a thought occurred to me, "I'll accept the truck on one condition; besides, I don't want you to kill someone because of me"

"If you ever think for one second that I won't take someone out for you, then you don't know me at all, now, what is it?" He asked as he held the truck keys out to me, almost as if no matter what I asked, he would do it.

I felt a little wicked right now and completely overwhelmed, "I want my name tattooed on you, and I want your name tattooed on me."

"I already had an appointment to get that done next week, so I'll see if I can change it." And the mic dropped.

I stood there floored, gaping I asked, "Seriously? You were already planning on doing that?"

"Yeah, why wouldn't I be?" How in the hell had I been this lucky to find a man like Knox? He surprised me every single day with another side of him that he has never shown to another soul.

Shaking my head to wipe the goofy grin from my face, I grabbed the keys he still held out for me as he pulled his phone from his pocket.

"Yeah. Fit me in today and my ole' lady?" I froze, he had just called me his ole' lady?

Without replying to whomever it was once he got his reply, he hung up.

"We gotta go. Going be a drive. Let's go."

I didn't move, how could I? "Ole' lady?"

He looked down at me as he grabbed a lock of my hair as he twisted it around his finger. "Yeah."

With an impish grin, I asked, "Do I get a property kutte?"

I watched his face soften just for me. Then he nodded.

My ole' man was a man of few words. I smiled to myself as I thought about that.

He placed a finger under my chin as he lifted my head, "What's that for?"

"You're my ole' man."

He laughed softly which was something new he had been doing as of late with me. With an arm thrown over my shoulder, we turned in his driveway, he walked us over to the behemoth white Ford truck, opening the truck door for me, I climbed in and settled myself behind the steering wheel.

I watched as he strode to the other side of the truck, when he climbed in he turned to me, "This feels fucking weird, don't expect this again."

I laughed; it did feel weird being in the driver's seat with him in the passenger seat.

I started my new baby up then set everything how I wanted it, after he gave me directions, we broke in my new truck with a five-hour drive.

And I had had a fucking blast. However, about two hours in, Knox had fidgeted in his seat so much that when I pulled into a gas station and told him to switch seats with me, his relief had been audible.

"You're a good driver sweetheart, but damn." I chuckled as he held open the door for me.

The moment we parked in front of the tattoo parlor, Knox jumped out of the truck, walked around the front of it, and opened my door.

With my hand in his we walked inside and I freaking loved it. All of the designs were amazing. The floor-to-ceiling beams were stained in a dark walnut.

"Knox, how's it going?" A woman called from behind the counter.

I looked at Knox to see that he had nodded at her, then he tilted his head, "Shiloh, this is my woman Fiona. Fiona, this is Miriam's sister and Dale and Lucy's adopted daughter, so to speak."

I nodded as I looked at Shiloh who had her mouth open, "He speaks? He speaks more than one word?"

I couldn't help but laugh, "I know. I guess I'm special."

"Yeah, this shit is crazy. Brother rarely even talks to me when I put ink on him." I looked to see a man at least a few years older than Knox. His hair was cut and it was close to his scalp. He had green eyes and ink all up his exposed arms.

He turned to Shiloh as he said, "I'll be tied up."

I also saw a kutte on him as well that was just like Knox's, only his had Tennessee on the bottom rocker instead of Carolina.

I also noticed that the woman seemed to have a crush on the much older man. That was going to be a fireworks kind of show.

We followed the man whose name I still didn't know.

The moment we walked inside his studio, Knox turned to me and said, "Fiona, this is Clutch." He tapped his crows on his arm.

Nodding, I looked at Clutch. "Your work is awesome."

"Thanks darlin'. So what ink are we doing?"

"Piece I spoke to you about." Clutch nodded.

Then he turned to me, "And you?"

I grabbed my phone as I pulled up the Apache symbol for love. "I want this over this area right here."

He took on the design, "Anything else?"

Looking up at Knox, I noticed that his face had softened, he brought his hand up and rubbed at the area where he had bit me. "You're mine, right?"

I saw his throat as he swallowed, when he nodded I turned to Clutch and said, "I want the initials, KSM, to be in one of the arrows."

I sat down as Clutch did my ink first and I fucking loved it. When it was finished and Clutch had placed a sheet of plastic wrap over it, Knox placed a kiss on it, and then he shrugged off his kutte, handed it to me, and then he pulled off his t-shirt.

I was curious to see what design he was getting and when I looked at it before Clutch placed the stencil on his chest over his heart, I gasped.

It was two crows, the wings were touching, and one of them had a king's crown on its head and the other had a queen's crown over it. I looked closer and saw that the design spelled out my name.

Standing there in fascination at the tattoo, I never imagined that this was what he had in mind. He had this all planned out.

As we were walking out Clutch said, "Wrath MC looks good on you." I tossed a smile over my shoulder.

"Looks good on you too." Knox growled, and I couldn't help myself.

"Hey Clutch?"

"Yeah darlin'?

"I love your tattoos, does that one on your arm expand to other places?" Knox spun me around and pinned me to the wall.

"Sweetheart…" He growled.

Smiling, I stood up on my tiptoes as I kissed the underside of his jaw right under his beard. "You have nothing to worry about."

Stepping out from under his arm I walked over to Shiloh to see her eyes on Clutch.

How much do we owe him?"

"Nothing." Clutch said as he walked up behind me.

After we said our goodbyes, since it was so late, I climbed in Knox's lap as he drove us home. Luckily, we weren't pulled over.

The moment we got back to Clearwater we headed home. And in the driveway, we broke in my new truck.

Two days later I was sitting on Knox's lap while a fire was going. It was growing colder in the months, and being up here in the mountains, it was even cooler. We had already consumed hamburgers and hot dogs. Drinks were steadily flowing.

Kida sat by my feet, and I had to turn down everyone's question if I would ever breed him and if they could get one of his puppies.

When everyone started to head inside due to the fire going out, I got ready to stand to do the same, until Knox squeezed my waist with his arm.

I turned in his lap to look at him.

He brought his other hand up to press his fingers to my pulse and to cover my tattoo.

"Knox, what is it?" I was getting worried.

He looked at me as he asked in a whisper, "You love me?"

I looked at him as I stared deep into his eyes. "Yes Knox."

"Words." He demanded.

I smiled as I bent and placed a soft kiss on his lips, murmuring, "I love you."

When I pulled away his eyes had been closed, and then he opened them. I could see concern and uncertainty in them.

"I'm shit with words Fi. But all I know is that I want you through thick and thin. You're the very air I breathe. I was spiraling down into a dark abyss the day I met you. You're my one treasure in life. The one thing that is all mine. Give me you for eternity. Marry me?"

I had to know something first, "If I ask you something, will you be honest with me?"

The uncertainty filled his eyes completely, when he moved to turn his head, I grabbed it with both of my hands and I rubbed his jaw. "Do you love me?"

When Knox didn't say anything, only stared into my eyes, I saw a lone tear come out of the corner of his eye. I leaned forward and kissed it away. The moment I leaned back I heard the words that I had longed to hear. "Yes Fi. I love you."

I didn't try to wipe the tears that trailed down my cheeks, "You're not shit with words, honey. Yes, a thousand times yes!"

As he placed a square-cut diamond that was set in a rose gold band on my ring finger I threw my arms around his shoulders, pressed my face in his neck as I let all of the tears flow freely.

"Sweetheart… you're killing me." I heard him say in that gravelly voice that I loved so much.

"I'm just so happy," I muttered through my tears.

His only reaction was to chuckle.

"Hey what's going on?" I heard Novalie ask as she must have stepped back outside to see what was keeping us.

Unable to reply, I pulled my hand from the side of his neck and showed off my ring.

With Novalie's gasp, I smiled through my tears, then placed my hand back on the side of his neck.

The next day while the men worked on the bikes the women talked about my engagement and how we were going to get married. I was surprised that they had almost everything planned in under fifteen minutes however, I wanted what Knox would want.

And I knew that he would only want it to be just us.

"Thank y'all for trying to help but I'll talk to Knox, see what he wants first." The ole' ladies simply smiled and none of them were bothered but what I had told them.

Within a minute after I told them that we were talking about what they had achieved and what they wished they could change.

Marley looked at me as she asked, "What's your greatest accomplishment in life?"

Softly I replied, "Giving myself to Knox."

And like the ever-present shadow he was, he walked up behind me, leaned in, kissed the side of my neck, and murmured, "Glad you did honey."

Then he laid something in my lap. I looked down at the white box, then tilted my head back.

After he kissed me he whispered, "Love you."

"Love you back."

I watched his fine ass as he walked into the clubhouse for church.

The moment the doors closed I opened the box, curious to see what was in there. And then I pulled away the tissue paper, I gasped.

Grinning like a kid at Christmas, I pulled out my property kutte.

"Woohoo!" Filled the air as all of the women congratulated me. Standing, I put it on and loved the softness of it. I bowed then spun around. The name said Property of Knox on the back above the club's logo of Lucifer and below that it had said Carolina.

"When do you want to get married?" I asked him as we sat on the porch swing the very next morning before I had to be at work, drinking our morning coffee.

"Don't want a big wedding sweetheart." He told me. "Long as you're there, don't care."

Biting my bottom lip I asked him, "Take me to Vegas?"

And that was how two days later I was married by Elvis to Knox Stephen McCord.

As I laid in his arms while I listened to his deep breathing, I ran my hand over the tattoo that he had inked over his heart. The rain was pounding down on the metal tin roof.

I couldn't help but stare at my ring and at the wedding band that was on his ring finger.

Had I known that this was where I would have ended up all those years ago, the only thing I would have changed was meeting Knox a hell of a lot sooner.

"The guy who takes a chance, who walks the line between the known and unknown, who is unafraid of failure, will succeed." – Gordon Parks

## Chapter 15

### Knox

I was brushing my teeth when something occurred to me. Over the past few weeks we had forgone a condom all together.

Since we had the birth control conversation we had decided to allow nature to take its course. Thankfully, because I had tossed every single condom in our bedroom in the trash. Those fuckers were torture compared to what it felt like ungloved in Fiona.

And I know that she hadn't had a period since we had gotten our tattoos.

Walking out of the bathroom with my toothbrush still in my mouth, I headed to the front porch. "Fi, have you had your period?"

She sat there with a raised brow, "Yeah, I had it…" Then when she trailed off her eyes grew wide.

"Get ready." I turned on my feet, finished brushing my teeth, and dressed.

Fiona was fidgeting with her hands. Seeing worry in her brow I walked over to her, placed my fingers under her chin and lifted until her eyes met mine. "I love you."

She smiled, "I know, I love you too."

Hand in hand we walked out to the truck, opening the back door so Kida could jump in.

Then we headed to the pharmacy. The entire drive over, Fiona kept looking out the window, moving her rings around on her finger.

"Sweetheart." I called softly to her. She turned her head to look at me, "Everything will be okay."

Tears formed in her eyes; I was wondering if this wasn't news that she wanted. "What?"

"It's just, I don't want you to feel trapped."

I looked in her eyes, "If I didn't want to be trapped, I wouldn't have your ink on me, I wouldn't have put my ring on your finger. And I damn sure wouldn't have made you my ole' lady.

The moment we walked down the aisle we stopped, "Which one?" She asked as she looked up at all of the options.

I reached out, grabbed one, handed it to her, then grabbed another one. Looked at the back of it to see how accurate it was.

The moment we made it back home, I walked with her to the bathroom as I carried the bag.

Opening the boxes we pulled everything out and read the instructions, "Oh I gotta pee."

She grabbed three tests, pulled up her skirt, and then she did what she had to do, handing me each test that I grabbed with a paper towel, I loved my woman, but not that fucking much.

Laying them on the counter while she finished I said, "Test takes three minutes."

However the moment she washed her hands I looked down and sure enough all three windows already had a plus sign in them.

She froze as she grabbed the box with her still wet hands, "One line is negative, and two lines is…"

Looking up at me with her eyes wide she said in a whisper, "Positive."

A breath-taking smile formed on her face, I bent over and wrapped my arms around her waist, lifted, and spun her around.

She placed her face on the side of my neck and giggled.

Sitting her on her feet, I placed my hands on her face, then I kissed her.

Dropping to my knees I wrapped my hands around her hips and placed a kiss on her belly, "Get ready little one. I hope you look just like your momma."

Placing another kiss on her belly, I stood, wrapped her in my arms carefully and carried her to the bed.

After making love to her and paying special attention to her belly, I started to make mental notes on things that needed to be done to the house. Baby gates. Locks for the cabinets, and doors. Alarms for all of the windows.

Shaking me out of my list was when Fiona leaned up on an elbow, "You ready for my question of the day?"

Fake sighing I said, "Lay it on me."

"How old are you? We are married and I don't even know that." She chuckled.

"Thirty-five."

Her eyes got a wicked look in them as she snickered, "Damn, your old."

Growling, I rolled atop her then tickled her. "No... Knox." Her laughter caused Kida to jump up on the bed and start licking the both of us.

Laughing at Kida, "You?"

"Twenty-three."

I looked over at her. "Not too shabby to have landed a hot young piece."

Her eyes narrowed, "Take that back."

Shaking my head, "Negative."

Angrily she bit out, "You'll take it back."

"What you gonna do about it?" I taunted her.

And when she winked, climbed off the bed and started to do a sultry dance, needless to say after her torturing me, and not letting me touch her while she danced. I ended up taking it back.

**Fiona**

A few hours later we headed to the department store, Knox was like a kid at Christmas and I found myself giggling every single time when he smiled and held something up.

He was going to make a great father, this thought had anger surging through my veins all because of his mother.

Knox had told me that he had no clue who his father was, he said that when he was younger and would stupidly ask, she told him that she didn't know.

I had plans to buy him one of those ancestry kits for Christmas so maybe if he had any relatives that had submitted their DNA we could find them. I still can't believe that he had agreed to it as long as I wanted him to.

As we were walking to check out with some basic essentials, he asked, "When do you want to tell everyone?"

"Let's wait until we see a doctor. I'll call when we get out to the truck and make an appointment with my OB."

And apparently that night, instead of getting morning sickness, I had nighttime sickness.

The entire time, Knox wiped the back of my neck with a cool cloth while he made sure none of my hair fell into the toilet bowl.

Seeing that I was sick, Kida nudged his nose in my knee and whimpered. Scratching his ears I had been about to tell him that I was okay, until more stuff came up that I didn't want to notice.

After I was sure that nothing else was going to come up, I flushed the toilet, then grabbed the mouthwash that Knox held out for me.

Soon as I was finished with that, he bent at the waist, wrapped me up in his arms and carried me to our bed.

"What have you got there?" I asked him as he grabbed something he picked up at the store earlier.

"Says it's for stretch marks and shit. Doesn't bother me, those are tiger marks, but I figured you would like to keep them to a minimum." Placing my hand on his cheek I grinned and nodded.

Sheepishly he ducked his head as he squirted some shea butter on my stomach and rubbed it in.

"Hey Knox, I don't want to know the gender, I want it to be a surprise." I looked at him to see him smiling.

"Fine with me. But I want to go over names." Laughing, I laid there as he massaged the lotion on my belly.

That night while I fell asleep, it was to the sounds of Knox talking to our baby.

That morning while we were eating breakfast before the appointment I said, "I'm going to try to find another job where I won't be on my feet."

"Why?"

"I don't know how much you make and you haven't let me help pay any bills since I moved in with you."

"Money isn't an issue. You don't have to work."

"Knox… seriously? I have to work. The baby will need things."

He pulled his phone out and two debit cards. "Was going to give these to you later today."

I grabbed the debit cards and saw my name on them, then I looked at his screen and gasped. "Knox.. what on earth?"

"Like I said. Money isn't an issue."

And that was when he told me about a boy he had met in juvie and how much he gets from Jacob every six months. He told me that Jacob had given him twenty percent of his company.

Just as we were about to head out, there was a knock on the door. No one ever came up here, Kida's hackles started and a low menacing growl emitted deep from his chest.

I watched as Knox walked to the door, checked it, then he opened it, "Yeah?"

"Hi, My name is Robert Caswell, I work with Peters, Rodgers, and Stein. I am here to discuss a great opportunity with you, may I come in?" I had to smother a laugh when the man actually tried to step up to Knox, thinking that he would move.

It wasn't Knox that responded, no it was Kida, he lunged and snarled at the man, watching the man's face turn white was pretty comical.

"No."

"It's extremely chilly up here." The man tried again.

"Not for sale." Knox said darkly.

"Well sir, it's more of an opportunity, you see…"

"No. Leave." Knox growled.

At Knox's growl when the man started to say, "But sir I…" Kida wasn't having it, he lunged for the man as he started barking, warning him.

The man fell backward off the front steps. Walking over to them I placed my hand on Kida's head, he calmed instantly, "We are not interested in selling, not now, not ever. Best you can do is to leave us alone. If you don't we will be contacting our lawyer for harassment." I didn't know if we even had a lawyer but I knew that was the only way to get them to leave us alone.

The man bolted to his car, he didn't even leave us a card, that would have been a good fire starter.

"We come to love not by finding the perfect person, but by learning to see an imperfect person perfectly." – Sam Keen

## Chapter 16

### Fiona

That morning Knox and I were sitting in the waiting room at the Women's Center while we waited to be called back. I was still floored at what he had shown me.

"Fiona McCord?" A woman in pink scrubs called.

We both stood, walking hand in hand, we followed her, all with the women sending lingering looks at my husband. They could look all they wanted, because at the end of the day, I was the one that got to lay beside him every night.

After the nurse got my vitals and had me pee in a cup we waited for the doctor to enter the room.

Knox took in the pictures on the wall and looked at me, 'I'll be by your side the entire time Fi. You hurt. I hurt." I looked at the picture that had his attention earlier, it was of the vagina and how everything worked.

"Love you honey."

It was then that there was a knock on the door. "Hey Fiona, good to see you again." I smiled at her.

"Good to see you too." Dr. Chase had been the one to run every single test known to man when I had left Cole.

She had the results in her hand, "Congratulations are in order, this early in your pregnancy we can't do the typical ultrasound but we can do it vaginally if you would like to see your baby?"

"Yes please."

"Alright, let me get the technician in here so she can do that for you. Undress from your waist down, you can cover up with this." Knox grabbed the cloth from her.

After she left, a technician came in with a machine. "Now this is going to feel weird but I promise it'll be over soon. Keep your attention right on this monitor."

With his hand in mine we did just that. And the moment we were able to see a black blob there on the screen I smiled wide. Then we both froze as the little thump-thump filled the room.

"That's your baby's heartbeat." She smiled wide at us.

"Knox, grab your phone, take a recording. I want to see if Clutch can tattoo that……. on me so we can use our phones to hear it anytime we want."

His smile had gotten even bigger as he did just that.

She printed off some pictures and handed them to me. "Congratulations."

"Thank you." I smiled.

"Dr. Chase will be in here in just a minute."

Knox had taken the pictures from me as he studied them.

When she walked back in she said, "Due to your husband's size and your smaller stature, we will need to keep a close eye on the baby's measurements as we go. I want you to take prenatal vitamins. Here is a little pamphlet of things you have to avoid and a list of medications that are okay to take. If you have to take any pain medication, take Tylenol only. Any allergies, Benadryl."

Nodding, I grabbed the pamphlet and saw that Knox still hadn't taken his eyes from the ultrasound.

"Any questions?" Dr. Chase asked.

That was when Knox lifted his head and boldly asked, "Sex?"

Dr. Chase smiled warmly as she answered, "Yes that is more than okay."

I looked at him in confusion, and like the badass he was, he proudly said, "Don't want to hurt you or the baby."

My eyes watered, every single time he allowed that side of him to be seen I just couldn't help myself.

"I see you did finally find a good one. And it was a question like that, that I'll know you'll make a great father. Congrats to you both." Dr Chase smiled as she walked out ahead of us.

"Thank you Dr. Chase, for everything."

"My pleasure. I'll see you again at twelve weeks."

The moment we got home, I took one of the ultrasound pictures and put it in a frame and sat it on the mantle next to our wedding photo.

Knox had been silent for the next few days. Which wasn't uncommon for him, but it was weird that he had barely said a few words to me.

Cotton had arranged for other clubs to come to the clubhouse to discuss a few things and opening up another chapter.

The moment we made it to the clubhouse I was a little worried about Knox. He hadn't said a word to me the entire drive.

After an hour of talking to the women and eating my ribs alone, I went in search of him. A lot of people were here for a meeting that the club had to have.

I spotted him leaned up against the fence outside with his back to everyone.

Walking up behind him, I wrapped my arms around his waist, I felt his muscles tense, and then his body softened.

Pressing my face in the gap between his back and arm, he lifted his arm so I could see what had his attention. Smiling when I saw that it was our baby's sonogram. The little black and white photo that he carried everywhere. If it wasn't on his person then it was set up somewhere where he could see it at all times.

He didn't care that I had one of the pictures hanging up in the living room. No that wasn't good enough,

"Okay?"

Softly I said "Yeah Knox, baby is happy. He loved the ribs."

Knox simply nodded, "Are you okay?"

I watched as he closed his eyes, took in a breath, and let it out. "Not really." He said quietly.

"Wanna talk about it here or at home?" I asked.

He wouldn't ever talk about things if he could be overheard. I remember something happening a few weeks back.

We had been at the clubhouse and they were hammering out some details with a new alley that they had established.

*A woman that had been talking to other people had made her way over to us and had sat down in a chair, not even asking if she could join us.*

*"So Knox... why do you have those black birds on your arm?" She asked as she made a move to finger one of his crows, Knox moved his arm out of her reach and placed it on my thigh.*

*"Crows." I muttered softly at his side. This woman was really starting to piss me off. She hadn't asked the ole' ladies things, only the men and she was already getting death glares from the women too.*

*"I didn't ask you honey fluff." Not only did my spine straighten but Knox had just gone from cool and calm to postal.*

*I tightened my hand on his that still rested on my thigh. "And I don't really care. You're not his mother, his wife, his lover, nor his friend, so really when it pertains to Knox, it's none of your business."*

*Nasally she said, "I'm just trying to get to know everyone."*

*"Why? You're not Wrath MC." I told her with a head tilt.*

155

"My husband's club and theirs are allies now, come on your too pretty to be stupid." It took everything I had to keep Knox's hand on my thigh at that comment.

"Again that doesn't give you the right to know anything about him or his brothers for that matter. You're not an ole' lady, you don't have a property kutte. Just because you have a piece of paper doesn't mean shit in this world, it's the leather on your back that matters, and it's the ink on your skin. And your damn lucky I have ahold of Knox's hand, you would've had a bullet in your head a minute ago for saying that stupid comment."

"I'm the wife of the president of an MC, how dare you speak to me in that tone."

"And I am the wife and ole' lady of Knox the Icer of Wrath MC. How dare you try to speak to him."

She turned her glare away from me then softened her look at Knox, "You didn't answer my question."

Knox had pointed to me. "My ole' lady knows."

"Well yes, that's all great and everything, but these are your brothers. How can they trust you if you don't tell them everything?"

"Brotherhood isn't built on that. It's built-on actions rather than words. Actions that show just who a man really is. And if you take another verbal jab at my brother and his ole' lady, ole' lady or not, you'll be thrown out of my clubhouse." I had wanted to clap, go Cotton.

The woman's man had walked over to her, jerked her up and pulled her out of the clubhouse. When he returned, she hadn't been with him.

Knox pulled me into his embrace, and yes you guessed it, he rocked my world with what he said next, "I'm terrified I'm going to fuck this baby up Fi."

I was aghast, "No you won't, because I won't let you."

He looked down at me, "Neither one of us has memories to draw from."

"That doesn't matter. We raise them how we see fit. Besides, we've got a whole club at our backs if we need it, they are raising some kick-ass kids."

When we returned back inside Cooper brought us over two beers, Knox grabbed one, and when he handed the other one to me, I bit my lip and shook my head.

Cooper froze, "You sick?"

"Not exactly." Peering up at Knox underneath my lashes, I smiled up at him when he did the same, it was then that he placed his hand over my stomach and smiled.

"Wait? Are you serious right now?" Cooper asked with a shocked expression.

"As a heart attack." Grinning Knox pulled the ultrasound picture out of the inside pocket that rested against his heart from his kutte and showed it to him.

"Holy fuck." He shouted.

"Cooper, what are you hollering about?" Miriam asked as she looked at what he was seeing and then she too turned wide-eyed at us.

"Pregnant?" And that was when the entire clubhouse quieted down.

"Yes we are six weeks along." I said proudly, Knox wrapped an arm around my neck and pulled me into his chest.

Hollers, catcalls, whistles filled the clubhouse.

"Guessing this means you'll be adding more crows to your arm if y'all have a daughter?" Cotton grinned widely.

I felt Knox tense. "No. I'll dedicate my leg for that one."

"Congratulations sweetie." Marley said first.

"It's truly a miracle." Lucy chimed in.

"I can't wait, I'm going to be the best damn aunt that baby has ever seen." Phoebe grinned as she looked at the ultrasound that the women were passing around.

"Get in line." Novalie told her.

"A tiny change today brings a dramatically different tomorrow." – Richard Bach

## Chapter 17

### Knox

When Cotton had told us in church this morning that a hero was returning from war today, his wife had reached out to us to see if we could offer him one last ride, we had all agreed.

Cotton walked out of his office "Mount up, a hero just returned home, he needs an escort to his final resting place." All at once we all stood, our women standing to walk us to our bikes.

I pulled Fiona into me and kissed her hard, "Be back."

"Be careful. I love you." She whispered as I bent my head to place a kiss on her stomach, "Be back little one. Daddy loves you."

"Love you sweetheart." Placing another kiss on the top of her nose I started up my bike.

The moment we made it to the landing strip, the plane was just taxiing.

We all parked, then got off, walked over to the doors where they would bring his casket out. I took the front right across from York. Cotton beside him, Xavier beside me. Garret took the back left with Cooper on the back right.

His wife had walked in front of us while we carried the casket to the waiting car.

Turning my head to see men and women with signs outside of the fenced-in area saying *You should die for what you did. You don't deserve this. No War.*

That had caused me to step from the car as I walked over there. I hadn't walked over there alone either.

"Leave now." I growled out.

"This is a free country." One woman had the nerve to say.

"Yeah because of that man's sacrifice. That man in that casket gives you that right. My brother standing right beside me, gave you that right."

"You think you can scare us off?" One little asshat said.

"Well what's the point of that when I can just remove you from this earth?" Garret asked them as he fingered the weapon under his kutte.

The moment I saw someone about to throw the American Flag to the ground I grabbed my piece from the small of my back beside my knife, and took aim, "You drop that flag, I'll drop you."

Luckily for the little shit, he swallowed and then handed it to someone else as he walked off, unlucky for me, I'd been in the mood for some new ink added to my arm.

When the others realized they were in danger, they all left.

"Thank you." The woman said as she wiped a tear with a tissue she had in her hand.

I nodded as I walked over to my bike after Cotton made the signal for all of us to load up.

We drove for two hours as people pulled over because of our escort and because of the American Flag that was flying out of trucks that were taking over the tail of the convoy.

After we arrived at the cemetery, we all took our same places outside of the car. The moment the door was opened, we each grabbed hold of the casket.

We carried it to the plot.

Standing there behind the row of chairs, Sergeant William Petty received a twenty-one-gun salute.

As the man in the dress blues handed the woman the folded-up American flag I looked to Cotton as I whispered. "Do more of these."

He nodded, then took in all of our brothers' faces to see the same look.

Just as I mounted my bike, my phone rang, seeing Fiona's name, I answered, "Sweetheart,"

"Hey honey, think we can have everyone over for dinner tonight? Usually we go to their houses, thought it would be nice." I could hear uncertainty in her tone.

Shaking my head, "Yeah that's fine."

I could hear excitement in her tone, "You sure?"

"For that smile I know you're wearing, yeah."

Then ever so softly I heard, "Okay. Love you. Hurry home."

"Love you." Hanging up I noticed my brothers were on their phones too.

The moment they all ended their calls, "Dinner at my place tonight."

"Bro, never been to your place." Xavier stated.

"Same here." Walker chimed in.

Cooper, the jokester said, "Finally going to see the bear cave. Right on."

"Fuckers. Just follow me."

We made the drive, and the moment I veered off to turn into my drive, I heard their brakes, ha, fuckers. Smiling a rare smile all the way up to my house.

My driveway had never seen this many vehicles nor bikes.

"Had I not seen you turn, I would've never known this was here." Cotton muttered.

"Yeah, peaceful, quiet, a bit isolated." As I said that, they all stared.

"You really do speak more than just a few words. Holy fuck bro." I wanted to smack Cooper upside his big ass head, only Miriam didn't deserve it.

Instead, I glared, "Thank my ole' lady." I muttered as I led them through the front door, just in time to see Kida bound over to me, "Hey bud, protecting mommy?"

He barked then he bounded over to my brothers. Had she not taken Kida around them at the clubhouse a few times, Kida would be a snarling mass of fur right about now. Just ask that developer that wanted to buy my property a few days ago.

Looking up it was just in time to see Fiona, walking down the hall with the women and the kids in tow.

"Hey honey," she murmured as she made it over to me, wrapping my arms around her I hauled her to me, lowering my head I kissed her hard.

"What's for dinner?" I was starving.

"Spaghetti, salad, and garlic bread." She smiled up at me.

"Like you made a few weeks ago?"

"Yes."

"Fucking A sweetheart." Grinning up at me I watched her ass as she walked into the kitchen and pulled out everything she would need to make her sauce. My woman didn't like the taste of the pasta sauce that was store-bought, so she made her own.

The only thing she didn't make was the pasta, and that was because she didn't care to learn how.

Kida was over in the living room on the floor, living his best life as all of the kids rubbed his belly and laughed every time his back leg kicked when they hit his sweet spot.

Walking to the fridge I pulled out beers for everyone, I knew that Fiona had stopped on the way home to buy them. Handing the beers off I got chin lifts in agreement.

"Y'all want a tour?" I asked them.

"If I could rewind and see this house again for the first time, I would do it." Phoebe sighed.

"Our place isn't good enough?" Xavier looked offended.

"Shut up, you'll get me after you see it." Chuckling, I led them through the house and out to the back deck.

After we returned Phoebe looked at Xavier, "See what I mean?"

He sniffed, "Maybe."

Grinning, I walked to the island, set my beer down and leaned into the countertop, resting my forearms there.

"What are you making?" Dale asked as he pulled out one of the bar stools.

"Homemade pasta sauce for spaghetti, salad, and garlic bread."

"Homemade?" I could tell he was grinning from ear to ear judging by his tone.

"Yes. The way it tastes in a jar, " she cringed. "Can't stand it."

"You need any help?" Pebbles asked as she walked over.

Fiona smiled down at her, "Yes, think you can open these two cans of tomatoes for me?"

"Yes!" Grinning, Fiona pulled her a barstool over then helped her up.

Pebbles had her tongue between her lips as she concentrated on her task. "Done. Look mommy, I helped."

"That's awesome sweetie, good job." Phoebe came over to check her progress.

"Now think you can pour them in this pot?" As Fiona asked her that, she grabbed the can and poured it all in the pot.

"Now we have to keep stirring it to make sure everything mixes correctly." She instructed. After a few minutes, Pebbles had grown bored with that, then with her mom's help, she was down and running to play with Kida again.

"Honey, will you pull out the extra leaf and set the table? Kids can eat at the coffee table." Nodding, I grabbed the plates and shit that we would need, Novalie, and Miriam grabbed them as I set them on the table while I grabbed the extra leaf.

"Need to put Kida up?" York asked as he meandered over.

"Nope, he won't mess with anything unless he's offered it by hand."

"Please tell me you plan on breeding him?" Cotton asked as he too took in how behaved and well-tempered Kida was.

It was then that she told him about the breeder where she got Kida from. He got the contact information.

Music was playing softly in the background as Fiona set all of the dishes at the table.

Once everyone was sitting and the kids were eating while a show they all liked played on the television, Fiona said, "We want to thank everyone for coming to our home. I want to personally thank everyone for what you have all done for Knox and welcoming me into your family. Now, let's eat."

"Holy fuck, what's in this?"

"Won't ever tell." She winked at him.

"Party pooper." Dale muttered around another forkful of pasta.

"But I will tell Lucy." Lucy smiled wide.

Dale shoved a piece of garlic bread in his mouth. "Good."

"Really good." Xavier muttered.

Rounds of agreements flowed. Laughter filled the space. My family was something else.

After everything was gone, literally, even though Fiona made a double batch, the women had helped clean up.

Lying in bed that night I curled my body around hers and placed my hand protectively over her stomach. I allowed her soft snores to lull me to sleep.

"Know that whoever is trying to bring you down, is already below you." – Boonaa Mohammed

# Chapter 18

## Fiona

Since the diner was only a ten-minute drive Knox had given in this one time and agreed to drop me off and pick me up on his bike for my very last shift at the diner.

I may have used a blow job to get my way but I had won.

A family came, when I made it over there to them I said, "Hey y'all I'm Fiona and I'll be your waitress. Can I start y'all off with some drinks?"

"Now see, this is why I want to move down here." The woman said. "Y'all are nice and I love the accents."

Smiling, I said, "Well, I wouldn't want to live anywhere else."

Just as I was taking their drink orders, I looked up to tell them something, and froze when I saw Cole and a woman on his arm. It was Stacy, she and I had been in the same grade in high school.

"Take a seat. Be with y'all in a moment." What I really wanted to tell them was to get the fuck out of here. Knox was definitely rubbing off on me.

After I sat their drinks down, got their orders to Randy, I walked over to Cole's table.

"Cole, what are you doing here?"

Without missing a beat he said, "Fiona, I made a mistake. I want you back."

I stared at him and gaped. For three seconds before I bent forward and laughed so hard I almost peed my panties.

"Cole, what are you saying? I'm sitting right here." Stacy waved her hand in front of his face.

Cole ignored her as his eyes locked on me. "It's not a laughing matter Fiona.

"Yes it really is. You honestly think I would ever take you back? Have you been drinking some strong ass kool-aid?"

"No, I miss what we had. I miss it all. I understand where you were coming from now, and I am fully capable of committing to that."

"Trust me Cole, whatever I saw in you is long gone. So far gone that I just pity you. You had a good woman in me. So good that had you cared just the smallest amount, you would've had gold."

His face turned red, "Pity me?"

"Yes, because there you sit with the whore of our high school and here I am loving life and so thankful for it.

Haughtily, Stacy stood from the booth, "Bitch, It's not my fault that men love my body."

Smirking, I said, "Love your body? Honey, you look like a fake, caked-up Barbie doll."

"I look good enough that I even took your man." Yeah the she bitch was out in full form today.

"Yeah, you did take that." I pointed at Cole, but then I smiled as I heard Knox's bike pull in front of the diner.

"But you see I'm good enough to get that." I smiled as I pointed at Knox when he just stepped through the doors to the diner to give me a ride home. Since today was my last day.

He ignored everyone in the diner as his massive legs ate up the distance in front of me.

"How's my baby?" He asked as he placed one of his big hands protectively over my stomach.

Sighing, I said, "Ready to let its momma get off her feet."

"Hey, you interrupted our conversation," Cole said nasally.

I watched Knox turn his head slowly to look at my ex, "Was that ass-kicking the first time not good enough for you?"

However before either man could say another word, I turned my head to the newest arrival that had just walked in the diner, I froze.

It was Sorcha, and she had what looked to be a three-year-old boy on her hip. I looked at the boy, then looked at Cole and muttered, "Only sleeping my ass."

At that Knox chuckled then winked at me with a smile.

I lived for those smiles. When he flashed one, nothing else seemed to matter. In fact I had been oblivious to what was happening until I heard something shatter.

I looked over and saw that Stacy had thrown her plate on the floor. "You've got to be kidding me."

"Sorcha?" Cole asked as he stared.

"Hi dirtbag. Meet your son." Sorcha said with a sneer.

I sat down on one of the barstools as Knox leaned against the counter with his arms crossed over his massive chest as he watched the entire show play out before us.

"Hey, Liv, mind grabbing me a slice of apple pie and some pickles?"

"Those pregnancy cravings, I don't miss those. One sec." She turned as she grabbed me a plate and set my slice of pie, and some pickles.

When I grabbed my fork, got a pickle and some pie, put it in my mouth, I moaned.

Looking over at Cole it was to see that his jaw was hanging open, "Your... your pregnant?"

"Yep. My husband has some super swimmers." I grinned as I grabbed another bite

"You married... that?"

"Sure did. And it was the best decision of my life."

"So you wouldn't give it to me, but you gave it to that piece of..." I dropped my plate on the counter behind me, stormed over, pulled my arm back and punched him.

"Don't you speak about him as if you know him. You don't know a goddamn thing about him. I thank God every single day for that man. He loves me. He cherishes me. You don't even deserve to breathe the same air that he does."

"Yes, we are moving down here." The woman squealed as she dipped another fry in her ketchup while she watched the entire thing unfold right in front of her,

"You told me you didn't have any kids." Stacy stared at the little boy in Sorcha's arms

"Well he wouldn't have had he not put something in my drink when I showed up to wait for Fiona."

Snarling, I was about to punch Cole again, until Knox wrapped his arm around my waist and pulled me to him, whispering, "Calm." Then he tapped my wrist over my crow.

Turning my head, it was to see the darkness in his eyes, I swallowed then nodded. For that act, Cole would be meeting his maker. And soon.

"I'm out of here. You creep." Stacy strode out of the diner.

Cole then ran after her trying to apologize. He was such an asshat.

Over the next few weeks, Sorcha and I had reconnected, she had told me that she didn't remember sleeping with Cole, but she did admit that she had felt off when she had awoken that next morning. I had already been at the diner when she had left all those years ago.

I had actually thanked her for opening my eyes somewhat. She had felt horrible but it really wasn't her fault.

A few days later I stood at the kitchen counter when there was a breaking news story on the television. Normally I didn't pay them any mind, not until I saw the picture that flashed up on the screen. It was Cole.

I turned my head to see my man that had just walked out of the nursery after hanging a drawing that Shiloh had made for us, over her crib. We were almost ready for our baby's arrival.

There on his left bicep was another crow.

I didn't like that he killed people. However what I did like was that my man wasn't afraid to take out the trash. And any man that would rape someone and use a drug to do it, well he was trash.

I walked over to him, smiled, stood on my tiptoes, and kissed him.

Then when I pulled away, his face had softened, I tapped the newest crow on his arm and winked at him.

However, I didn't make it far from him. He wrapped his arms around my waist, pulled me to his front, bent, and placed his face in my neck as he whispered, "Love you Fi."

"Love you too Knox." I whispered right back.

Just as I had done that, there was a knock on the door. Kida immediately walked over to the front door and growled.

Knox stepped around me, checked the door, then he flung it open, "Jacob."

"So this is what you spent a small amount of that money on?" I raised a brow at Knox. Curious as to who this person was, was this the same Jacob that he had told me about?

"Suits me." He said as he stepped aside and allowed him to enter, at that move Kida quit growling but he padded over to me and placed himself between me and the man.

"And who is this?' He asked as he looked at me with Kida at my feet.

"Fiona. My wife." Knox stated proudly.

I saw his jaw drop at that. "Why didn't you invite me to your wedding?"

I couldn't help the chuckle that came out, "We eloped. My man isn't for big crowds."

"Fiona, this is Jacob, this is the man I was telling you about."

Smiling, I walked over to him and hugged him, I whispered, "Thank you for always having his back."

When I pulled away, he looked down at my belly, his eyes grew wide as he turned his head to glare at Knox. "And y'all are expecting and I didn't even get a fucking phone call?"

"Brother…"

"I know how you are Knox, hell if you were on your deathbed you still wouldn't call."

"Well I'll call you from now on." I reassured him.

"Good. You better." He said angrily.

"So let me ask another question, I tried to send you your check, only it came back. Want to tell me why it came back because you now have a middle name on your account?"

Knox looked at me with so much love in his eyes, "Fiona."

Jacob then turned his head, looked at me with an amount of respect, then said, "You ever need me, you call. Don't give a fuck what it is."

And that was also how I learned that Jacob was actually Jacob Alexander Cleland, one of the richest men in the world.

Turning my head to see Sorcha walk in through the back door with Saxon holding on to her finger I smiled. When I turned my head back to the men it was to see Jacob's eyes locked squarely on her.

Well then…

"If she's amazing, she won't be easy. If she's easy, she won't be amazing. If she's worth it, you won't give up. If you give up, you're not worthy. ... Truth is, everybody is going to hurt you; you just gotta find the ones worth suffering for."
– Bob Marley

# Chapter 19

## Knox

Watching Fiona's belly grow every day with my child was something of a miracle. Every month we took pictures with Kida showing the progress.

When she had been five months along, the breeder had contacted her that they had a female that was ready so we drove to Virginia to allow Kida to mate with her.

Luckily in three days' time, that was all it took. However, while she was talking to the owners they were amazed with Kida and the connection he shared with Fiona that they had ripped up the contract and offered one of their females to us so that the breed could be expanded, we would be picking that female up after our baby was born.

And that was how Fiona went from working in a diner to being a registered breeder and running a program. A program that Jacob had backed and had found us the top dog trainer to train the puppies for special needs. whether the dogs needed to alert their handlers for seizures, blood pressure dropping, panic attacks, and anxiety attacks.

Sorcha had finally settled in Clearwater with Saxon and wouldn't you know it that Jacob flew to Clearwater not only to see us, but to see Sorcha and Saxon. She was giving the man a run for his money.

Three months later the owners in Virginia, sent us pictures of Kida's first litter of puppies.

We were sitting with our doctor going over the birth plan and everything, since it was time to choose.

"I want a natural at-home birth. Even though we don't know who my people are, the Apache did this all the time."

I wanted to argue with her. Tell her that I wanted the best in the field to take care of her and our baby, but it was her call. I would be there all the way.

"Your call sweetheart."

"Then you'll need a midwife, and I'll be here ready and able if god forbid something happens."

And that was how an hour later we had a midwife.

The nursery was ready, we had gone with a white crib, a white dresser, with warm colors for the bedding things Fiona called accents.

Now we were just waiting for our baby. The midwife had told us that once Fiona hits thirty-six weeks the baby could come at any time. We had just hit our thirty-seven-week mark. It was about to become all surreal for us.

"Sweetheart?" I had just stepped in the house after taking out the trash to see Fiona with her hand on her stomach at the sink.

"These contractions are no joke. I thought those Braxton hicks contractions were strong, but these…" She had been complaining of back pain all morning.

"Do I need to call Helen?" Helen was the midwife we had chosen.

At Fiona's nod I did just that. Helen answered on the second ring, "Hey Knox."

"Contractions."

"Has her water broken yet?"

"No."

"Okay, I'm about thirty minutes away, be there soon." Then I went to the bedroom, stripped the sheets off and laid down what we would need so that the mattress wouldn't be ruined.

Walking back out to the kitchen it was to see her breathing in and out with Kida keeping pace beside her.

Sending out a text to my brothers that it might be time for our baby to arrive.

"What do you need Fi?"

"Washcloth." Nodding, I grabbed her one, ran it under cold water and then I pulled her hair up in a messy bun as she called it and placed the washcloth on the back of her neck.

Within minutes, the roaring of pipes could be heard as they came up the mountain.

Walking to the front door I opened it, then I walked over to Fiona as I wrapped an arm around her back as I walked with her, she stopped, then doubled over, her arms going to her knees.

It was then that I saw liquid rolling down her legs and hitting the floor. "Got it." Cooper said as he went straight to the paper towels and grabbed a trash can.

"Thanks Cooper." Fiona breathed out.

Grabbing my cell I walked Fiona to the bedroom, after I helped her down on the bed I called Helen, this time, she answered on the first ring, "Water break?"

"Yes." I stared down as Fiona breathed through what had to be another contraction.

"Fifteen minutes away."

"Y'all need anything?" Novalie asked as she walked into the bedroom.

"Can you…. can you grab the things in the chair over there and place them on…. the bed."

"Sure." She grabbed the blankets and the things the midwife had said she would need.

"I texted Jacob, he's on his way." She told me as she breathed through another contraction.

It was then that I heard Helen walk through the door. Phoebe entered with Helen on her heels.

"Let's check you out sweetheart." Since Fiona had on a wrap day dress Helen climbed on the bed and checked her over.

"You're already eight centimeters dearie. Won't be long now." Helen climbed off the bed then she checked her blood pressure.

"Novalie, Phoebe, can y'all stay in here with us please?" Fiona asked. They had both agreed wholeheartedly.

Over the next hour sitting there on the bed with her, my heart was breaking, she was being so strong and battling everything like the warrior queen she was. We were on five hours of active labor now after her water had broken.

The brothers had been walking in and out checking on things. The other women, Sorcha included, had been in the kitchen making us meals for the next few days.

Then suddenly Fiona said, "I need to... I need to push."

Helen smiled then said, "Okay, let's check you out dearie."

Helen climbed in the bed as she checked, then looked up with a smile, "It's time, I can see the head. Okay, Knox, can you grab her leg and hold it up, Novalie can you grab the other?"

After Novalie and I had Fiona's legs, Helen turned to Phoebe, "Phoebe, can you get a blanket ready?"

"Okay Fiona, with your next contraction, I want you to bear down with your bottom and push until I tell you to stop, okay?"

Fiona nodded while sweat beaded up on her forehead. I saw her face tighten and then she started to push. She yelled out while she did it, "That's it sweetheart."

"Good Fiona. Keep pushing." Helen did something and then she said," Okay stop."

Fiona tipped her head back as she breathed through the pain. This was fucking killing me.

"What can I do?" I asked her with sorrow etched in my voice.

Turning her head, her eyes softened, "You're doing it honey."

I leaned down and kissed her temple.

"Here comes another one." She said suddenly.

"Okay… push…" Helen called out.

"Shoulders are out."

"Fuck this hurts." I saw tears come out of the corners of her eyes.

"One more push Fiona. Push as hard as you can." Phoebe had the blanket ready.

"Ughhhhh…." And then I heard it, the sweetest sound filled the room.

My child had just entered this world. Turning my head to look at it, "You have a beautiful baby girl." Helen had grabbed something then looked at me, "You want to cut the cord?"

Nodding, but first I leaned in and kissed Fiona, "Thank you my love."

Her smile was breathtaking as I pulled away and cut my daughter's chord.

After Helen had her wrapped and swaddled she handed her to Fiona.

While Helen was cleaning everything up, I lifted both my girls in my arms while Novalie, Phoebe, and Lucy stripped the sheets from the bed as they replaced it with clean ones.

Carrying her to the bathroom I held on to my daughter while I helped Fiona into another wrap dress so she could breastfeed easily.

Once that was done, I carried her back to the bedroom to see our makeshift family in the room, I laid them back in the bed so she could rest.

Cotton stepped closer so he could see her, "Well what's her name?"

Smiling down at my girls I said, "Please welcome Kiiri Alea McCord."

"She's beautiful brother."

Giddily Cree clapped, "I was right." She smiled as she held a little pink gift bag out to me.

Grabbing it I smiled, opened it, and pulled out a pink onesie with the word's *Icer's Princess* written in black ink.

"Fucking perfect Cree. Thank you." I told her as I showed it to Fiona.

181

Grabbing my daughter I brought her little head to my lips as I placed a kiss on her forehead, she was so tiny that she didn't even span the length of one of my forearms.

"I'll let Clutch know to be on the ready for my ink." I growled.

Even though I knew Fiona was wiped, she still tossed her head back and laughed.

The room filled with chuckles at my comment. I fucking meant it too.

That night while Fiona lay beside me sleeping, I couldn't help but place Kiiri on Kida who hadn't left her side at all since the moment he padded into the room.

Pulling out my phone I snapped the picture.

"That's going on the mantle." Fiona said drowsily.

After the two of them were checked at the hospital for their twenty-four-hour check-up to ensure both of my girls were healthy, we drove to the clubhouse for a welcome home celebration that Novalie had thrown for us.

Since we were also having an all-welcome celebration later on in the day so that more members of the community could see who we were and what we were about, the place was jam-packed.

Glancing up after everyone had welcomed Kiiri home, it was to see Fiona walk out of the kitchen. I was sitting there with Kiiri in my arms when I caught some assholes leering at her.

Where they fucking oblivious to the property kutte she had on and the giant as fuck ring on her finger?

Then my baby girl Kiiri woke up and apparently wanted her momma. Holding her protectively in my arms, the moment I made it to Fiona I handed her Kiiri then I turned and glared at the stupid little dumb fucks.

"Honey…" I growled as I turned my head to see Fiona chastising me with a look.

"Don't honey me sweetheart. I get they want to look at you. I know your fucking breathtaking. What they are not going to do is disrespect you by undressing you with their eyes. Cause if they don't stop, I'll pop their eyes out of their sockets."

When one of the little boys scoffed at me, I slowly turned my head, and advanced.

Wrapped one hand around his neck and squeezed.

"Feel that?" I could see the capillaries in his eyes start to bust.

His face started to turn purple.

Growling I said, "Look at her one more damn time."

As soon as I let go, the other little punk that was with him, grabbed him by his arm and dragged him out of the clubhouse.

An hour later Fiona sidled up next to me, looking up at her I could see that she was tired, "Ready to head home honey." She was worn slap out. A lot of the women had been amazed that she had elected for a home birth and hadn't, not once, asked for any pain medicine.

Ten minutes later blue lights were coming into the driveway.

An officer stepped out, put his hand on his gun as he made his way over to where we were standing.

"Got a call about an assault. Boy claims you almost choked him to death. Here to take you in." I looked at his name plate, it was Goldman.

But before anything else could be said, my woman spoke up, making me want to spank her ass.

"He's mistaken, he didn't want to admit that it was a female that almost choked him out, he shouldn't have been leering at me like that and eyeing my daughter in my arms." Fiona said without urgency, and without a stutter.

The officer took in her small stature as she held Kiiri in her arms, "That the way of it?"

"It sure is. The boys kept eyeing my daughter as well." Phoebe walked up with Pebbles at her side.

"That's right. It was creepy." Pebbles even shuttered.

It took everything in me to not bust out laughing. This cop was putty in all of their hands.

"Well then, in that case, I think it was justified." The cop nodded as he walked off, climbed in his car, and left.

"I gotta watch you." I chuckled.

She winked, "No one takes you from me."

"Miss Fiona is right Uncle Knox. You are ours." Pebbles said around her lollipop.

"As you move toward a dream, the dream moves toward you." – Julia Cameron

## Chapter 20

### Fiona

Two months later, I had just fed Kida and Kaya the female Lycan Shepherd that we had received and was pleased that Kida was being extra attentive to his mate. However, the moment they were full, they broke apart. Kaya went to rest outside of the nursery. Ever since we had brought Kaya home, she had made it clear that she was loyal to Kiiri.

Kida had stayed with me when I walked to the nursery, peeked my head in to see Knox with Kiiri in his arms as he rocked her to sleep, singing softly to her.

Over the last two months we had come to a routine. I would get up with Kiiri to feed her and if she wasn't tired, Knox would always walk in the nursery to rock her until she fell asleep.

Smiling I left them to their daddy-daughter time as I made myself a cup of coffee and made my way to the front porch swing. Kida jumped up with me as he laid his head in my lap.

About half an hour later, Knox walked out with his own cup of coffee just in time to see Jacob coming up the drive.

Smiling at him my jaw dropped as I saw Jacob round the car as he helped Sorcha out of the car, and then he helped Saxon out who immediately held his hands up for him to carry him.

"So you finally gave in?" I smiled at Sorcha.

"Yeah he has a way about him." She said as she sighed at the vision of Jacob holding Saxon.

"Daddy... spin." Jacob laughed as he spun Saxon around.

"Daddy?" Knox rumbled out.

"Yep." Jacob grinned happily.

"Happy for you brother." Knox nodded at him.

Sitting with Sorcha in the backyard she asked me, "Saw the news, Cole was killed."

I lifted my decaf coffee to my lips and looked at her. "Something you want to ask?"

"I've seen killers. See it in Knox."

"And?"

"He the reason Cole is dead?"

I stared at her, "Not sure what you're talking about."

She smiled ear to ear, "Yeah you do. Tell him thank you."

It was then that I felt his presence walk up behind me, "Welcome." He handed Kiiri to me.

After they left I had just laid Kiiri down for her nap. Just as I walked in the front door Knox's phone pinged with a text, he looked down at it then he put his phone back in his pocket.

Walked over to me, and whispered in my ear, "Dove."

"Be careful. We love you."

He grabbed the back of my neck with his hand and kissed me hard.

As I watched him walk out the door I knew that I would always be proud of what he did, even though it meant that it took him away from us at times.

Five months later, walking into the clubhouse after I dropped off our newest adoption with Kiiri in my arms I had a surprise for Knox.

The moment I spotted him, I smiled at him, walked up to him, and then pulled the pregnancy test out of my back pocket.

He shook his head as he did the same thing that he had done when we found out we were pregnant with Kiiri. There in the middle of the clubhouse, he dropped to his knees as he placed a kiss on my stomach and muttered., "Mommy and daddy love you."

Nine months later we hadn't been able to do a home birth due to the size of our second baby. Kase Graham McCord had come into this world at nine pounds and five ounces.

Thirteen months later we welcomed our last addition to our family, Kynnydee Felicia McCord, and I was able to have our last child in our home.

Jaya, Kiiri and Kida's son from their first litter had formed a connection with Kase.

Two months later we had made the drive to pick up another set of Lycan Shepherds, Toko and Tamala. Toko was about twenty pounds lighter then Kida and Tamla was almost the same size as Kaya. It had been Toko that had bounded with Kynnydee.

"We're all a little weird. And life is a little weird. And when we find someone, whose weirdness is compatible with ours, we join up with them and fall into mutually satisfying weirdness — and call it love — true love." –
Robert Fulghum

# Epilogue

### Fiona Three Years Later

While I sat on my ole' man's lap in the backyard for Kiiri's birthday party I had to stifle a laugh. Our girl was all girl, much to her father's amusement. And there with her new Barbie dolls and her new horse figures, Maddox sat with her while he played with her.

Knox looked over at Cooper and said, "You payin', or am I?"

"What do you mean?" Cooper asked after he took a pull from his beer.

"Wedding." Knox said as he nodded over at Kiiri and Maddox.

Cooper dropped his head and placed a kiss at Miriam's temple then said, "You're the father of the bride, so it's on you, but I'll cover the alcohol."

Knox brought his glass of Jack to his lips and muttered, "Good."

I smiled down at him, kissed his lips, and before I could lose myself in my man's kiss, our other son and daughter came over with their Aunt Phoebe in tow.

"Mama mama mama." Was babbled as I bent to pick up Kase, set him in my husband's arm then I bent and grabbed Kynnydee.

"They may not have had too much cake. Sorry but not sorry. Payback for when Knox gave my two kids two giant as fuck chocolate chip cookies before bed time last month." We had watched Bash and Pebbles so Xavier and Phoebe could have a date night.

Even though Knox told them not to tell, it was Pebbles that had ratted him out to her mother.

I heard Knox groan. Smirking, I kissed Kynnydee's head.

Jacob swooped in and stole Kase from Knox grinning as he spun Kase around. When Knox had asked him to be Kase's godfather, I had agreed wholeheartedly.

\*\*\*

Eight years later as I sat in a restaurant with my brood and my husband I couldn't help but smile at what life had given me.

"Momma, I'm going to get a refill." Kase said as he grabbed his cup.

"Okay baby." I watched as he stood, he had gotten a lot better at that. He had on shorts today because he wanted to show off his new prosthesis that Shiloh had painted. It was an exact replica of Knox's gas tank.

I fucking loved it. When I had tried to pay her she had just stared at me with a raised brow.

However in the next instance I watched some little girl look at him, then she pushed him when he stepped forward. Before I could get to him, my daughters were up and out of their seats.

The girl was laughing and calling my boy a gimp, I had seen red.

Knox stood and then I followed. However, I was smiling all the way over there because I knew my daughters.

**Knox**

"My momma didn't raise no bitch; you don't put your hands on my little brother." Kiiri snarled.

"And you most definitely don't make fun of him." Kynnydee snarled in her five-year-old voice.

I stood there as my two daughters got in the face of a girl who thought it would be funny to push my son down and laugh at him. My son had suffered an infection when he had been riding on his bike down the mountain and hadn't seen the log until it had been too late. The bike had rolled on his calf causing it to break. Sadly, the bone never healed and an infection had set in, we had done every single therapy and every single medication known to man, but it hadn't been enough. So at seven years old, my son had a below-the-knee amputation.

And before I knew it, Kiiri pulled her arm back and punched the girl straight in the nose, the sound it made filled up the restaurant. Everyone had stopped eating to watch the exchange

It was then that a woman who was wearing too much perfume walked over and yelled, "Your daughter broke her nose."

"Then you need to teach your daughter some fucking manners. She made fun of my son and she pushed him when he took a step which caused him to fall. Maybe if you were a better parent you wouldn't have an asshole of a daughter." Fiona snarled.

"Do you know who I am?"

"No and I wouldn't give a damn even if you were the queen of England."

"You'll hear from my lawyers about this." Before Fiona could respond, I pulled my phone out and texted Jacob.

"Good, and you'll hear from my lawyer. And rest assured, before my lawyer is through with you, you'll be living in a cardboard box." Fiona grinned daringly.

The woman put her hand on her hip and glared. "I'm not afraid of you."

When my phone rang I glanced at it and saw that he was calling, "Why do you need my lawyer?"

"Some little bitch shoved Kase when he took a step, fucking laughed and called him a gimp. Kiiri and Kynnydee saw it, then Kiiri said her momma didn't raise no bitch and she slugged the girl in the face. The little bitches mother is threatening to sue."

"They fucking wish. Tell them who my fucking lawyer is. No one fucks with my godson."

Nodding, I hung up, glaring at the woman I asked, "You heard of Lance Davidson?"

"Who hasn't? He's like..." I watched as her eyes widened.

"Yeah bitch, he's going to eat you for lunch." Fiona grinned.

And then all three of my kids at one time said, "Chomp."

Fiona then turned to look at our kids, "Lesson of the day, you ever say bitch again before you turn eighteen I'll wash your mouth out with soap. Furthermore, that was a fine hit." Fiona smiled as she turned and walked out of the restaurant.

All the while patrons were clapping as the woman still stared wide-eyed.

Needless to say, we didn't need a lawyer. No because Jacob had been enraged and had gone after the little girl's parents. In fact they had to sell everything and donate the proceeds to the Wounded Warriors fund because that was the cause that Kase had chosen.

When he had turned five he had told me he wanted to join the military. Unfortunately because of his accident he would never get that chance.

However, fourteen years later Kynnydee stood in a room as she swore in, in honor of her brother.

I never thought I would have kids before I met Fiona. To be honest I had been scared shitless, to raise a baby when I didn't know fuck all about it, and neither did Fiona. But my woman, she stood at my side the entire time and guided me. We didn't follow any rules, we just raised them as we saw fit.

And yes both of my girls had a foul mouth when the need arose for it, but I always saw Fiona smiling proudly when they handled themselves.

A young man walked over to Kynnydee in his uniform and asked her why she joined.

She smiled as she pointed at Kase, "Because this was his dream, and it's my honor to do this for him."

And as I watched Kase, Kiiri, and Kynnydee hug, I felt so much pride as I stared at my kids.

However, just as another boy in a uniform approached Kiiri, it was Maddox that stepped in his path and glared at him as he shook his head. Luckily, Kiri wasn't so much of a girly girl anymore so her wedding wouldn't be breaking the bank.

I always thought that Fiona was my chance at Redemption. But it wasn't only Fiona, no it was my kids as well.

They were my Redemption.

The End.

## Note From The Author

It is with a heavy heart that we are about to say goodbye to these men and women. I enjoyed creating their stories and I hope that I have done them all justice.

I must say that Clearwater's Redemption is my favorite of this entire series.

But they are not completely finished. A special Christmas compilation will be coming out and some questions will be answered in that book. Hint Hint.

I wanted to thank each and every one of you that bought one of my books, that took time out of your lives to read one of their stories. For those of you that have reviewed them, messaged me, and stuck by me this entire time, Thank You from the bottom of my heart. I wouldn't be able to do this without y'all.

# Connect With Me

## My Website

Home - Author Tiffany Casper (mailchimpsites.com)

## Facebook

https://www.facebook.com/authortiffanycasper

## Instagram

https://www.instagram.com/authortiffanycasper/

## Goodreads

https://www.goodreads.com/author/show/19027352.Tiffany_Casper

# Other Works

## Wrath MC

### Mountain of Clearwater

Clearwater's Savior

Clearwater's Hope

Clearwater's Fire

Clearwater's Miracle

Clearwater's Treasure

Clearwater's Luck

Clearwater's Redemption

Christmas in Clearwater (December 2021)

### Dogwood's Treasures

Dove's Life

Phoenix's Plight

Raven's Climb (August 2021)

Falcon's Rise (September 2021)

Lark's Treasure (October 2021)

Swallow's Grace (November 2021)

Wren's Miracle (January 2022)

Crow's Forever (February 2022)

New Year Special (TBD)

**DeLuca Empire**

The Devil & The Siren

The Cleaner & The Princess (TBD)

**Novella's**

Hotter Than Sin

(Free eBook on my Newsletter)

Silver Treasure

The Rancher's Heart (TBD)

Made in the USA
Middletown, DE
18 February 2025